DIANNE'S DESTINY

Winona Bennett Cross

Dianne's Destiny
by
Winona Bennett Cross

Publisher/Distributor:
The Open Rood Books, LLC
1942 W. Locust
Durant, OK 74701

ISBN# 9781732006119

Cover Design: Virginia McKevitt

Published in the Unites States of America

Publishing History: First Edition Print 2023

Note:
This novel is a work of fiction. Names, characters, places, and incidents are either the product of the author's imagination, or, if real, used fictitiously.

Dedication & Acknowledgements

This book is dedicated to the real Dianne, her high school sweetheart and husband, Sam, and her family.

The main character of Dianne's Destiny, Dianne Jacobson, was based on Geneva Dianne Ringener Morrow, one of my dearest friends from high school.

Throughout her life, Dianne left love and joy in her wake. She always put family, friends, and God first, had a great sense of humor, and was accepting and available.

She loved horses but hated chickens.

The beautiful character on the cover closely resembles Dianne. Many hearts broke when Covid took her home.

Rest in Peace, My Dear Friend.

Geneva Dianne Ringener Morrow

November 6, 1950-December 11,2020

Author's Note: Dianne's Destiny was my first book and was originally published in 2014 with The Wild Rose Press as part of a series. I couldn't think of character names so friends of mine became the characters.

Many of them will recognize themselves.

I got my rights back and have rewritten the book with several edits and changes and without the focus found in the series. I hope you enjoy Dianne's Destiny. If you do, please consider leaving a review. ~ Thank YOU!

Special Thanks To:

Pamela S. Thibodeaux for being a friend of my heart, for believing in me, and for finding mistakes I didn't know I made.

AND

Virginia McKevitt Thank you for the gorgeous cover of Dianne's Destiny. Breathtaking is a common word, but so appropriate.

Chapter 1

Butterflies swooped and tumbled in Dianne Jacobson's stomach. She parked her red SUV in the parking lot at Horses of Hope Equestrian Therapy Center, then slowed her breathing. Sweat ran in rivulets onto her forehead and down the back of her neck. She wiped it away with a used napkin from the floor of the car and slammed her palms on the steering wheel. A few months ago, she was a confident professional woman. But now, the recent inability to control her actions frustrated her. *Breathe, Dianne, breathe.* Dr. Murphy's voice echoed in her mind. *Inhale, two, three, four. Hold, two, three, four. Exhale, two, three, four.*

Dianne repeated the process until her heart and mind calmed, then made her way into the therapy center's office. No one greeted her from behind the reception desk. She glanced around the empty waiting room, chose a seat, then flipped through the pages of an ancient magazine without reading a word. Agitation mounting, she tossed the periodical aside and glanced around.

On the wall, an array of photos featured smiling men and women alongside beribboned horses. Large and small trophies reminded her of soldiers standing at attention. The center's mission statement, framed with gray barn wood, hung above the desk.

Dianne read it and frowned. The benefits of equestrian therapy seemed unrealistic, but she had agreed to follow the doctor's orders.

A young woman bounced into the office and flashed a blinding white smile set off by hot pink lips. Her blue eyes sparkled. A thick, shoulder-length blonde ponytail swung from side to side, filling the room with the scent of vanilla and brown sugar. "Hi! I'm Beth Kelso. You must be Ms. Jacobson. I was checking on your horse."

"Yes, but please call me Dianne." She stood and shook Beth's hand but avoided eye contact.

Dianne took the purple clipboard and feathered pen Beth handed her, and worried the receptionist's bosom might pop the pearl snaps on her white western shirt. Neon pink boots with turquoise insets accentuated Beth's flippy, short denim skirt. *Pink boots. I really am back in Texas.*

Filling out paperwork had become a chore. Same old questions, same old routine. The words blurred. *Coming here and being around other people is more than I can bear.* Dianne wrapped her arms around her midriff in a hug as panic filled her being. Her vision blurred. Chest tightened. Tears filled her eyes.

Beth sat down beside her.

"I'm sorry. I'm so sorry. Just give me a minute." Panting, Dianne held up her shaking hands.

"Don't worry about it." Beth handed Dianne a tissue. "Let's forget about this busy work and get to the barn. You'll feel better when we get out there."

The young woman's quiet compassion overwhelmed her. A new bout of tears fell. She turned, wiped them away, and blew her nose before following the perky receptionist to the barn.

Inside, the smell of hay and horses immediately triggered memories of happier times. Dianne inhaled the dusty, sweet scents and allowed the tension to wash away. She rubbed a palm over the spot where a flicker of hope ignited in her heart. Other than the ones forced to pull carriages day after day in Central Park, she hadn't been this close to a horse in fifteen years.

Beth pointed. "That's your horse, Emperor. Isn't he gorgeous?"

Passing several stalls where more of the beautiful creatures rested and waited, Dianne looked up to see her horse standing in the walkway. "Big. And beautiful." She halted mid-stride on her way to the tall, copper-colored horse with a flaxen mane and tail. Something about the cowboy whispering into Emperor's ear made her heart stumble, then lurch as though it had been shot out of a circus cannon. Something about the way those jeans fit him seemed familiar. And enticing. *Good Lord, what am I thinking? This is crazy.* She tried not to stare but couldn't look away.

Beth's voice interrupted her. "Wait here. I'll introduce you to the ranch manager. He volunteers his time and horses."

Dianne fidgeted in her boots and jeans. She longed for the designer suits and shoes that cloaked her in poise and self-assurance. Power clothes…that's what her friend Jocelyn called them. She used to be confident. She'd once found joy in volunteering and using her Sociology Degree to help the less fortunate. Now, meeting someone new made her anxious. She must be getting stronger though, as she hadn't bolted. *Yet.*

The cowboy came toward her, his fawn-colored hat pulled low. Sun-streaked brown hair fell over the collar of a chambray shirt. Her gaze lowered to his scuffed, worn boots and the 3G brand tooled into the bottom of his chaps.

"Hello." Dianne whispered and took the cowboy's outstretched hand. She forced herself to look up and take in a breath, then started coughing. She bent at the waist, clutching her stomach. This can't be happening. *Kip! My God! It's Kip.*

"You all right?" Kip reached to steady her. She hadn't heard that voice in fifteen years. Nor had she forgotten it. She glanced up to see recognition dawn in his eyes.

She waved him away. "I'm fine." Forcing herself to stand straight, she willed the faked composure to convince both Kip and Beth, who stood nearby—an obvious show of support. She pushed the hair from her face with a familiar, saucy flourish, but found she still couldn't make eye contact. The bravado lasted only a moment before her shoulders slumped and she stepped away.

"Are you sure you feel like finishing up out here?"

Dianne accepted Beth's hand on her back. Her actions must puzzle the receptionist.

She nodded.

"This is . . ." Beth held out her hand and gestured toward the cowboy.

"We've met before, Beth," Kip interrupted. Reaching into his pocket. he drew out three sugar cubes, which he offered Dianna hand out flat, palm up. "Hold them like this so he can't bite you."

"I remember." The brush of her fingers on Kip's palm sent shockwaves to her stalled heart, and the disloyal troublemaker burst to life, racing far faster than was good. Sugar cubes in hand, she walked slowly to the horse. Her breathing slowed. Moving away from Kip relaxed her in some small way.

Emperor's ears pointed toward her. He nickered and reached for the treat in her flattened palm. His musty but clean scent, soft muzzle, and unconditional acceptance calmed her in a way no therapy, conversation, medication, or relaxation technique ever could. She held the horse's face in her palms, looked him in the eye and saw trust. Running one hand alongside his neck, she moved to his side and buried her face in the coarse hair of his mane.

The resultant flood of cleansing tears surprised her. Dianne wept for the ambitious and frightened girl who ran away from home and a once-in-a-lifetime-love all those years ago. She found the success she sought. Happiness, on the other hand, proved elusive. Now, she was home again, broken in almost every way, and crying into the neck of a horse.

"Let's finish your paperwork." Beth took Dianne's elbow and gently led her out of the barn.

Dianne turned to search for Kip. He worked at the far end of the barn, grooming another horse. Sadness weighed heavily in her chest. She touched her heart with the tips of her fingers, wanting to feel its steady rhythm. She'd accepted the blame for the end of her relationship with Kip and her friends years ago. But they didn't know that. Her emotions see-sawed between anger and despair. Once again forced to squelch the knowledge that her choice to leave had been the wrong one, she swallowed the tears gathering in her throat and moved toward the office with Beth.

* * * *

Kip took a deep breath when Dianne left the barn. The woman he'd met today wasn't the dreamer he had fallen for. She was just as beautiful as ever, perhaps more so with the wisdom of maturity.

10

Oh, the rage he felt when he'd read the referral from Dianne's doctor and learned she had been mugged and beaten. He wanted to get his hands around the neck of the man who'd assaulted her. Willing away the ache starting to brew in his temples, he massaged them with shaky fingertips.

He returned his attention to the animal even as visions of her betrayal moved through his mind like a movie reel. He brushed the flank of the horse so hard the animal swung around and nipped at him. "Sorry, Boy."

Flashbacks of happier times flooded his memory. First kiss, for both of them. Funny, he could still feel the softness of Dianne's lips. The taste of her cherry lipstick. His heart had pounded so hard, he feared it would burst. Breathing practically stopped.

He rubbed his eyes with fisted knuckles and gulped hard to dislodge the knot growing in his throat.

Kip looked at the back of his left hand and rubbed the scar running from his thumb to the knuckle of his ring finger. They had been in an ATV accident. Dianne suffered a broken leg and was left with a long, jagged cut on her right thigh. Stupid kids. Typical teenagers thinking they were immortal and had it all. But the accident had opened their eyes to the fragility of life, and brought them even closer.

He pushed the sweet memories aside as the vision of Dianne leaving filled his mind. He could feel her cold palms on his cheeks, hear the anguish in her apologies, taste the bitter disappointment as she turned and walked away. He could still see the red glow of her taillights mocking him. He never knew why she left without warning only days after graduation.

"I'll be damned." Kip turned, kicked a feed bucket, and fled the barn as anger and frustration slammed into him with brute force.

"Beth!" He stormed into the office. "Give me Ms. Jacobson's folder. I need to know when she's coming again."

"Good grief, Kip. What bee got in your bonnet?" Beth slapped the folder into his hand. "Since when do you care about the schedule?"

"Not really interested in the schedule." Kip snarled and tossed the folder on the desk, leaving a trail of papers on the floor. "I need to know when to have Emperor ready. The farrier is coming next week."

The sharp puncture of Beth's blue eyes shooting daggers at his retreating back swung him around to face her.

"Stop glaring at me. I can feel the knives between my shoulders." He stomped out.

An hour later, he was back at the ranch. Stopping at the barn, he barked at his foreman to unload the horses, then covered the hundred yards from the barn to his back porch in record time. In the kitchen, he surveyed the rough-hewn walls, granite counter tops, and red color scheme. *Dianne would love this. Hell, of course she would love it, she practically designed it. Why is she back? After so long. And never a phone call or letter.*

Why hadn't he found a lasting relationship since she left? Of all the women he had dated, how come nothing stuck? Even Beth. He glanced around the room and in an instant knew the answer—because no other woman was Dianne. No one else even compared. No one captivated him the way she had from the moment he laid eyes on her in high school. He walked to the sink, splashed cold water on his face, and vowed to stay away from the equestrian center on the days Dianne was scheduled to be there.

* * * *

Dianne rubbed her grumbling stomach. She drove toward her hometown of Waurika, Oklahoma–a thirty mile drive northeast of Wichita Falls. Fried catfish, hush puppies, sweet tea, and lots of tartar sauce had been served on the Oklahoma side of the Red River for years. Crossing the bridge reminded her of the days she and Kip would sneak off with their friends to ride four-wheelers on the soft, shifting sand in the river bottom. She chuckled at the memory and rubbed the scar on her right thigh. Light flashing from the windows of a large log house on the bluff of the 3G Ranch distracted her and forced her to veer to the shoulder. She stopped for a moment and gazed at the home before easing back onto the highway.

The tires of her red luxury SUV crunched on the gravel. The sign at the roadside café was the same. Inside, little had changed. She stood in the entry, giving her eyes time to adjust to the dim light. An older waitress zoomed past her balancing a tray steaming with hot baskets of food and nodded at Dianne. "Sit anywhere, hon. Menus are on the table."

She chose a booth she last sat in fifteen years ago and tossed her lambskin handbag across the torn red vinyl to the far side. The menu remained the same, except for the prices. Though higher now, they were still cheap compared to those in New York. Catfish came in a half or full order.

A waitress put a basket of hot hush puppies on the table. "What can I get you, hon?"

Dianne smiled. "I'll have a full order of fish, fried crisp, and sweet tea."

"Enjoy your hush puppies. Your order will be up soon. You look familiar. Are you from around here?"

Here we go. This is what I've been dreading. Dianne fiddled with a loose strand of strawberry blonde hair then tucked it behind her ear. "I used to live here but left after I graduated high school."

"Yeah, what's your name? I've lived here all my life." She snapped her gum and cocked her hip as if she planned to stay a while.

"Geneva Jacobson." Dianne never believed she would be grateful to use her first and former married name. She hoped to discourage conversation and spread the napkin in her lap, repeatedly smoothing out the folds. A familiar, dreaded tightening in her chest signaled a pending panic attack. She slowly drew air into her lungs.

"Full order up." The waitress shouted in the direction of the kitchen. "I don't recognize your name but I'm not as young as I used to be."

Dianne watched the waitress cross the room in three strides and enter the kitchen. She puffed out her cheeks and exhaled in relief as her gaze roamed the room, seeking the familiar squeeze-bottle of tartar sauce. A basket of fish and fries landed in front of her, accompanied by a plate of onions and pickles. She groaned with appreciation. "Could I have tartar sauce please? There's no bottle on my table."

"Well, hon, the health department made us quit leaving it on the table like we used to. Now we just put it in these little cups. Here you go."

The crunch of corn meal fried golden brown, the light taste of the fish, and the first fried food she'd had in years exceeded her memory. A tinge of guilt made her think she should be more forthcoming. Each step toward starting over seemed to take more conscious effort than she ever imagined. She smiled. "Tastes as delicious as I hoped it would. You might remember me as Dianne Raborn. I graduated in 1996. You look familiar to me as well, but I'm not good with names."

The woman slapped her thighs and belted out a belly laugh. "Well, good Lord, of course I remember you. I'm Teresa Starling's mother. You girls used to keep me on the edge of my seat."

Dianne shook her head at the coincidence. "Really? You look great. I guess we did play havoc with you and my mother. How is Teresa?"

"She's just fine. Married one of the Howard boys. They have three children. Two girls and a boy. Have you seen Kip since you got back? He never married."

Dianne's heart lurched. Not trusting herself to speak, she nodded and dipped another piece of fish into the cup of tangy tartar sauce.

Mrs. Starling kept talking. "Do you remember Mr. Grant from the 3G Ranch?"

"Yes."

"When he died, he didn't have any more family. So, he left the 3G and everything he owned to Kip. After all, Kip's dad was the foreman before him. He'd practically been raised on the ranch." Mrs. Starling took a deep breath. "Did you see the log cabin on the bluff?"

Dianne nodded.

"That's his new home. Ricochet is Kip's foreman. He and his family live in the old homestead."

"It's a lovely house. The sun bouncing off of the windows nearly blinded me when I drove across the bridge." *Kip lives on the 3G, in that gorgeous home.*

The bell rang again. Mrs. Starling handed Dianne a note she'd scribbled on a guest ticket. "I have to get back to work. Here's Teresa's number. Give her a call."

* * * *

When Dianne left the fish house, she drove through her former home town. *Waurika, Oklahoma. Small Town, USA.* Memories assailed her. Sadness rose and left a lump in her throat as she drove by several boarded-up businesses on Main Street. A turn past the high school brought Kip to mind. She stopped in the parking lot, lowered the window, leaned out, and looked up at the statue of the school mascot. Funny, she remembered it being larger. The marquee announced homecoming, at which her alma mater would be playing a long-standing rival.

Images of games floated through her mind. She saw red and white dominating the bleachers, heard the cheers, and remembered the worry she felt when Kip was on the field. Even tasted the saltiness of the popcorn. She drummed the cadence of the school's fight song on her dashboard, surprised she remembered it.

Chapter 2

Fatigue hit hard when she arrived at her new home. "It's Dianne, Miss Wood," she called to the current owner of the historic mansion where she'd rented a suite.

Miss Wood came into the foyer wiping her hands on her apron. "Hey, Dianne. Did you find the Equine Therapy Center ok?"

Dianne nodded. "Yes ma'am. GPS led me right to it. Wichita Falls has changed a lot in fifteen years!"

Miss Wood grimaced. "The joy and pain of progress."

Dianne laughed. "Yes, ma'am."

"One more thing. Make yourself at home. Feel free to roam about and to use the larger fridge in the kitchen also."

Dianne thanked her hostess and pulled herself up the dark walnut stairs. She stopped once to enjoy the fresh, citrus smell of lemon oil that reminded her of Saturday cleaning with her mother. Every weekend, the two of them scrubbed their small house from top to bottom with lemon oil and Spic and Span.

Reaching the landing, she leaned over to admire the two-story Italian marble fireplace in the formal living room. The faces of mythological gods carved on its surface fascinated and reminded her of Rome. A large floral arrangement of coral roses and baby's breath dominated the entryway. She turned and walked into her grand suite. Relief washed over her when she locked the door.

The nostalgia of the day tugged at her heart, and Dianne found herself pulling out a box of treasures from her childhood. Things she hadn't looked at in fifteen years but felt compelled to bring with her. Tangible bits of memories she couldn't bear to part with. She pushed and pulled three boxes out of her closet and sat on the floor beside them. Which box contained exactly what she wanted?

Why didn't I have the foresight to write more than 'books' on them?

The first contained textbooks and certificates from her years of humanitarian service. Dianne shoved it aside, along with the next, with its collection of novels. Process of elimination completed, she reached for the one that held her memories and dreams.

She stacked photo albums at her side until they tilted precariously. To prevent a disaster, she straightened them, then lifted the red-and-white high school yearbooks out and opened them one at a time.

Making a desk from a soft, plump sofa pillow, she leafed through the class photos. She saw herself staring at and defying the photographer's inane effort to make her smile. *Being a teenager and having a father in prison had been hard.* The shame she carried weighed on her every day. The other kids were relentless in their teasing and bullying. Most of them believed she used drugs because of him. She swore *never* to take drugs because of him.

She was naïve in so many ways despite living with a drug addict and alcoholic. Kip came to the rescue when a group of bullies cornered her the day after her dad was arrested. *I guess he really did save me. Deep down I wanted to show the group of cruel kids that I could rise above my father and make something of myself.*

Dianne shook her head, hoping to banish the tears that crowded her chest and rose to her eyes. A sob she had held inside for longer than she cared to think about, burst from her in a harsh, insistent wail. She held the yearbook to her chest and rocked back and forth.

Her mother had received a cancer diagnosis at the beginning of her senior year. *God, I miss her.* Kip stayed with her every day. She would never have survived the loss of her mother without him. Fifteen years had passed since her mother died but Dianne still tried to call her any time she needed guidance. Just yesterday she ached because grief came out of hiding.

Dianne brought her fingers to her lips and kissed them, then touched the image of young Kip. She would forever be grateful to him for befriending her when she'd needed a friend more than ever. Neither of them expected to fall in love. Now, he was back in her life again…helping to save her and he didn't even know it. He should have hooked up with that cheerleader, the prettiest one whose father was a doctor. What was her name? It didn't matter. Dianne never believed she was good enough for Kip Mahan. The day she saw Kip horsing around with that girl led her to accept the scholarship back east. She convinced herself leaving would be best. Hiding her doubts became second nature. The dual fears of failure and losing Kip had come alive when she was alone at night.

She opened the yearbook from her senior year. It's musty smell reminded her of libraries and regret. There they were, smiling and mugging for the camera but always together. Upon seeing the next photo, Dianne swallowed hard against the stubborn lump growing in her throat. Tears filled her eyes. Senior prom, such a bittersweet evening. It marked new beginnings and the beginning of the end. Kip had told her each time they danced how much he loved the simple blue voile dress she wore. *He said it matched my eyes.*

She had known even then that moving east was an option she should consider, but kept the knowledge to herself. There'd been no lack of interest in her from universities. She was embarrassed, yet flattered, when she was voted Most Likely to Succeed. *And I did...but I paid a huge price. More than I can bear, it seems.* The small-town outcast became accepted, even popular, because of the love and kindness of a young cowboy.

Dr. Murphy had been right about the equestrian center. He told her—even ordered her—to visit. Perhaps it would help her overcome the debilitating panic and anxiety she had fought since the attack. Being near a horse had been comforting and cathartic.

Dianne decided to ask Beth at her next appointment if she could spend more time with Emperor. She wanted hours, not minutes. Would Kip be there?

Mrs. Starling said Kip had never married. Was it possible he still loved her? Or had her betrayal—when she left without warning—broken his heart into so many pieces he'd lost the ability to love or trust?

Dianne stretched out her legs, laid back, and cradled her head in cupped hands. Thoughts seesawed from past to present. Confusion reigned over other emotions. She knew the time for a confrontation of some kind would soon arrive.

Betrayal hardened hearts more than hatred, loss, or disappointment ever could. Life was offering her another chance for redemption. She no longer felt like she needed to run away. Everybody made mistakes, but hers had caused more harm than most. For the first time, she found herself asking why. Why had she never made a real effort to resume contact with any of the people from her past? Especially Kip. Somehow, making it big didn't seem as important these days as she once believed. The bitterness of guilt and regret rose in her throat. She pushed the yearbooks aside, stood, and stretched her back. She pressed a hand on her stomach when it growled.

Dianne stepped through the heavy, leaded glass door onto a small balcony where a masterpiece lay before her. Dusk hues of red, orange, and gold settled on the Texas plains. The horizon seemed endless. Putting her hands on the rail, Dianne leaned over, looked in every direction and imagined how the area must have appeared when the mansion was built at the turn of the century. A railroad lay within a few hundred yards of her balcony. The thought of the original owners being able to catch the train so near their home if they wished to travel fascinated her.

Sirens jerked her from the musings. The shrill sounds set her on a mental spiral back to New York. Tension built in her chest. She hurried inside. Time to talk to her one true friend—the only person in the past fifteen years who knew about Dianne's father, the death of her mother, Kip, and the real reason she left town.

Using speed dial, she called Jocelyn Hartford in San Francisco. When she answered, Dianne heard the shuffling sounds of paper and phones ringing. "Hey, sorry about the time difference. Do you have a minute?"

"Sure, for you always. How's it going?"

"Better. Every day is still a struggle, but I feel stronger. I think. I went to the equestrian center for the first time today. Had a couple of panic attacks, but being near horses again calmed me somewhat." Dianne heard the tremble in her own voice.

"Really? What else is going on? You seem upset."

Dianne hesitated before speaking. "Kip was there."

"What? Did you say Kip? *The* Kip?"

Dianne laughed at Jocelyn's surprise. "Yes. *The* Kip. I recognized him immediately. Seeing him triggered an embarrassing attack. He recognized me…I don't know how I feel about that. He looks damn good."

"What do you want to do, Dianne? Have you figured out how to deal with it?"

"I'm going back as scheduled and I've made a note to ask for more appointments. I'll do just about anything to get better, and my new doc believes in equestrian therapy. My verdict is still out. What are the chances you could take a few days off and come out here?" Dianne twirled her hair around her index finger.

"I'll see what I can do. Can you see me in cowboy country?" Jocelyn chuckled.

"You'll be the prettiest cowgirl around." Dianne smiled at the mental image. "Thanks, J. Love you."

A weight lifted from her shoulders knowing Jocelyn would be flying out as soon as possible. She would talk to her about the restlessness in her heart. She hadn't told her she had been thinking about moving again since she saw Kip. He'd seen the weaknesses she bore and that shamed her.

She put the three yearbooks on the mantle and repacked and moved the other boxes to the closet. Taking a bottle of water from the refrigerator, she headed to the bedroom. *Funny, I feel relieved after the meltdown and the trip down Memory Lane.* Within five minutes she had washed her face, pulled on a night shirt, and crawled between the flannel sheets. She settled in, then reached for her Kindle. Reading time.

Chapter 3

Dianne put her left foot in the stirrup and pulled herself over the horse's back with a groan. She wiggled her bottom into the seat, made sure her boots were properly set — heels down, and settled for a relaxing ride in the sandy arena. Urging Emperor into a trot, she allowed her fears to fly away behind her.

Horses healed the heart and soul. For reasons she no longer recalled, she had smothered that great truth. She hadn't seen Kip since the first day more than a month ago, but she knew he was around because a 3G truck and trailer was parked behind the barn. She looked for him everywhere. Traffic lights, the grocery store, the arena, McDonalds. Everywhere. His presence, real or imagined, dominated her thoughts.

She dismounted at the barn and led Emperor to his stall. He nudged at her and tried to reach the treat in her jeans. Laughing, she stopped and pulled a sugar cube from her pocket. "Here you go, greedy boy."

The horse laid his head across Dianne's shoulder, giving her the equine version of a hug. She squeezed his neck, scratched his ears, and gave thanks for this horse and his ability to heal people.

Softly humming Faith Hill's version of "Wild One," she brushed the now dozing gelding.

"You seem to be getting along well with Emperor."

Dianne gasped, dropped the brush, and spun around. "Kip! You startled me. I didn't hear you come in."

"What was that song you were humming? Sounds familiar." Kip patted Emperor's neck.

Heat rose in her face. She would hyperventilate if she didn't slow her breathing down. The brush of his sleeve against her arm left her skin breaking out in a range of gigantic goose bumps. She sucked in a breath to gain composure. "What? Humming? Oh, just a song from the nineties. You probably couldn't recognize Happy Birthday if I sang it. I've never been able to carry a tune."

Kip's hazel eyes crinkled at the corners with amusement. "Sounded like 'Wild One.' Our song."

Caught, Dianne just stared and tried to work a way out of the corner she had painted herself in.

Kip rested his arms on the gate to Emperor's stall. "Let's talk. I've tried to stay away or just be busy when you're here. I'm tired of that. We have to acknowledge each other. You're right. You still can't carry a tune."

Dianne pulled her arms across her chest and nodded.

"You don't have to be afraid of me, our memories, or the future." Kip's voice was soft, almost a whisper. He reached over the gate and squeezed her shoulder. Pushed a stray lock of hair from her eyes and tucked it behind her ear. Then he turned and walked away.

Dianne watched him leave. She had opened her mouth to try to speak before it was too late, but no words would come. Hoping busy work would calm her, she shook the dust and hair from the blanket and put the saddle on the rack. Afterward, she cleaned the bit and bridle, fed Emperor, and filled his water bucket. Holding her hands straight out in front of her, she bit back a groan at their pronounced tremble. Frustrated, she stuffed them in her pockets and headed to the office.

"Gracious, Dianne! Are you all right? You're so pale." Beth moved to assist her into a chair, then hurried over to the small fridge behind the counter.

Dianne accepted a bottle of water and gulped it down. "Thanks, Beth. I had a small panic attack, but I'm better now. I'm heading home for a hot shower, pizza, and a good book. Kip came to the stall. I guess he makes me nervous."

"He seems to be nervous around you too." Beth raised one eyebrow. "And that's odd. I've never known him to be anxious about anything."

* * * *

Kip's heart filled with something he hadn't experienced in a long time. Hope. Coupled with anger, yes, but hope nonetheless. He wished Dianne would laugh like she used to and throw her startling smile his way. A late afternoon breeze whispered through the wrap-around porch. He propped his boots on the rail while his mind pistoned up and down.

His foreman, Ricochet, walked toward him. "Hey, Kip. How's it going? Just thought you'd want to know your favorite mare will be foaling soon. Wanna walk to the barn with me?"

The chair and his bones creaked when he stood. "Yeah. Come in. I need to change. Wan'na beer?"

Ricochet nodded.

Kip moved to the refrigerator, handed the other man a bottle, opened one for himself and took a swig. "Be right back." Five minutes later he returned to the kitchen wearing his shabbiest jeans, oldest boots, a baseball cap, and a torn country music concert T-shirt.

"Have you seen Dianne lately? Is she doing better as far as those panicky things go?"

"I saw her, even tried to talk to her, but she had one of those attacks. I'll tell you this, I think that damn horse is better than any medicine those docs give her. You should see her around the arena. She sits a horse well. God, she's still beautiful. Well, let's go check on that mare." Kip took a draw from the long neck bottle, tossed it into the trash and started walking to the barn with Ricochet.

"What do you mean you tried to talk to her?"

"She froze up. I don't know how else to explain it. I'm going to be there in that stall with Emperor when she gets there the day after tomorrow. We have to face each other and talk this ghost out sooner or later." Kip put both hands over his face and scrubbed at it. "She has to know I'm on her side."

"Agreed, but be careful. I'm not sure I could save you again. I worried that I wouldn't save you when she left before. How's Beth acting? Does she know about Dianne?" Ricochet matched Kip stride for stride.

Kip shook his head. "Beth doesn't know anything about Dianne and me. I think Beth wants more from m—."

A screaming whinny spilled into the air. Both men broke into a run toward the foaling shed.

Patches, Kip's favorite brood mare, lay on her side heaving and sweating. She nickered at the cowboys as they knelt beside her.

"Hey there, Girl. Something wrong this time?" Kip looked at Ricochet. The muscles in his face knotted and tightened. Did his skin look as mask-like as it felt? "How long?"

"Not sure exactly. One of the hands brought her up to the shed three hours ago. I'll get Doc Brookes out here." Ricochet pulled a cell phone from his back pocket.

Kip turned his cap backward and caressed the mare's head and face. "Shh, it'll be all right. I think you might need a little help with this one." He cooed and whispered, trying to calm the mare when another contraction wracked her. He rubbed his hands over the contours of her body, trying to discern the position of the foal.

Reaching her flanks, he addressed Ricochet once more. "Did you reach the doc? This foal is in position. I think he's just a big 'un. Is the chain ready?"

"Doc's on the way." Ricochet kicked some straw out of the way and handed Kip the long-armed exam gloves.

Waiting for the latest contraction to abate, Kip pulled on the gloves, preparing to check the size and position of the foal. The mare whinnied, lifted her head, then dropped it to the ground.

Ricochet kept a comforting hand on her side. "Another one starting, Kip."

Kip pulled his hand and arm back. The metallic smell of amniotic fluid and blood mingled with the sweat of man and beast. "This little guy is front hooves forward for sure. He's close. Won't be long now."

Two hours later, with the help of the vet and a pull chain, they delivered a healthy colt. Patches was up and nudging her colt to his feet and nourishment. She licked him dry while he struggled to stand on weak, spindly legs.

Kip and Ricochet stood side by side watching mother and foal, beaming like new fathers pointing at their newborns through a nursery window.

"Look at that guy. Wonder how much he's gonna weigh?" Ricochet asked.

"Too soon to tell. He might be solid black except for that white star. Could get some hefty stud fees out of him in a few years." Kip poked Ricochet in the side. "You hungry?"

"Sure. How about a big steak with all the trimmings? Your treat?"

"You're on." Kip chuckled then rewarded Patches with a coffee can full of sweet feed along with a flake of hay. He quickly brushed her down and felt for hot spots that might indicate blood clots in her legs.

* * * *

"Damn good steak." Kip cut another piece of his ribeye.

Ricochet nodded and smiled.

"I'm not sure how this is going to work out with Dianne being home. I can't stop thinking about her. I've considered asking her on a date, but I chickened out. I can't go through losing her again. Other than to accept that high-dollar scholarship, I still don't know why she left. What do you think?"

"Well, I don't blame you. But I think you should find out more about what's happened to her over the years." Ricochet pushed his empty plate to the side.

"Yeah. That's going to be hard if she can't talk to me without having one of those panic attacks. Beth said she seems to be getting better."

"What would you do if Dianne told you she was sorry for leaving? Would you listen? Are you ready to deal with that?"

Kip leaned back, looked down, and lifted one shoulder. "I don't know. I still have a lot of anger when I think about it all. I thought I was moving on with my life. Now I'm drowning in memories."

Full and sated the friends paid for the tab, left the restaurant, and headed to the ranch. Kip sped down the expressway. He braked, changed lanes, and pulled to the shoulder. "That's where she lives." He pointed toward an apartment complex and a mansion.

Ricochet pulled a toothpick from his mouth. "Who?"

"Dianne."

"She lives in those apartments?"

"No. She's living at the mansion. Beth said she leases part of the upstairs. Do you remember having dinner there our senior year? None of us had ever seen such nice things. Our roots showed, didn't they?" Kip reached across and chucked Ricochet on the arm, laughing at the memory.

"I imagine Dianne got used to fine things in New York. Mama said she lived in a million-dollar condo, but you know how she exaggerates. Wonder how Dianne's adjusting?"

"That mugging sent her running home. Must have been harder on her than anyone believed. She's lost her confidence and avoids making eye contact, but when she does those blues of hers could make any man falter. The panic attacks scare me. I don't know what to do." Kip's words ended in a sigh.

He pulled back into traffic. They spent the remainder of the drive in the kind of comfortable silence only longtime friends enjoyed.

* * * *

Kip arrived at the equestrian center early to check on the horses. The quiet of the morning had always been his favorite time—the only part of the day when he could think without the interruption of phones, clients, or business.

A big mug of coffee in hand, he lounged on a bale of scratchy hay—for almost two minutes. Then he raked his fingers through his hair, stood, and paced the walkway between the stalls. *Maybe I'll invite her to Junior's for pie. Coffee and dessert seems safe and noncommittal.*

Beth swooshed into the barn, filling the air with the scent of lilacs. "Kip! Good morning. How long have you been here?"

"Couple of hours."

Questions flashed in Beth's eyes. Her perfect skin had been further enhanced with whatever women put on their faces trying to look natural, and she'd pulled her blonde hair to the side in a loose braid that draped over her right shoulder. *She's a beauty. Always smells so good. And boy, can she two-step! Dances the Texas Swing like a pro. What's wrong with me? Any other cowboy would fall for her in a heartbeat.* Heartbeat. *That's the problem. She doesn't make my heart race. Not like Dianne did, or like it does now that she's back.*

"Did I forget something?" Beth fiddled with a long angel-wing necklace she wore over her T-shirt, flashing a sequined flower down one sleeve. She cupped his face in one well-manicured hand.

Kip gently removed it, gave the long fingers a little squeeze. He met her gaze and shook his head—a discreet gesture no one but Beth would notice, even though no one else was around. He wouldn't play games. Not with Beth.

He cleared his throat and gnawed on the piece of straw between his teeth. "Nah. I just needed to do some thinking."

"You've seemed preoccupied. Can I help? Maybe I'll dance it out of you Friday night." Beth laughed, turned, and left the barn with a backward wave.

He watched her go. *At some point, I have to tell her it's no good between us. Not anymore. Maybe there never was anything there.*

Taking a moment to massage the ache in his temples, Kip wondered when and where would be a good time and place for something like that.

Well, no time like the present.

He cursed the voice of his conscience and headed toward the office. "Can we talk?"

A flash of something raw and primitive sparked in Beth's eyes. She arched a brow. "About?"

"Us."

"Oh, there's an 'us'? News to me."

Kip tilted his head back and closed his eyes. "No. I guess there isn't. That's what I wanted to talk to you about."

She held up a hand to halt his words. "Not necessary. I see the way you are around, and about, Dianne. Guess I've always known the couple of dates we had would never amount to anything."

"We have a long history that ended badly. Unfinished, really. But I am sorry if I led you on in any way. I never meant to."

She sighed. "You didn't. Foolish me thought I could break through that wall you've built around your heart. Now I understand why I couldn't."

"Thanks. Friends?" He held a hand toward her, surprised when she took it.

"Always. And don't worry. Knowing this doesn't change the way I feel about Dianne either."

Her smile warmed his heart and eased his mind.

Chapter 4

"I'm doing better, Dr. Murphy. The meds seem to be helping, but being around horses helps more." Dianne sat across from her trusted doctor. As always, he put her completely at ease. Today even found her in a rare, good mood.

Dr. Murphy turned a graph toward her, pleased to point out that she hadn't had a major reported panic attack recently.

Dianne blinked, surprised to see, in black and white, how much she had improved since beginning equine therapy.

"Have you considered more social activity?" Dr. Murphy reached for a peppermint. He offered one to Dianne.

"Do you have chocolate in that drawer? Lloyd keeps chocolate in his drawer." Dianne tilted her head and pointed to the left side of the desk.

Dr. Murphy smiled and opened the drawer. "With or without nuts?"

"With, of course." Leaning forward to take the candy bar, Dianne grinned. "I've made some progress and joined a monthly book club. Tomorrow I'm going to get out early and visit some estate and garage sales. I need a few items for my suite. It's furnished really pretty, but not with *my* things. I left so much behind in New York."

"Good for you. Does it make you anxious to plan these outings?"

"Not as much as it used to. I keep medicine in my purse. I know it's a crutch, but just having it calms me. I only get really nervous when I see Kip or if I'm put on the spot. Hopefully, going to some anonymous sales will help. What do you think?" Dianne settled back in the chair and crossed her legs, then began working at the candy bar wrapper.

"How often are you taking the meds for anxiety?"

"I usually take one just before I go to the center. And often before bed."

"It's good that you're going to be getting out. But why do you think it still bothers you to be around Kip?" Dr. Murphy uncapped his gold fountain pen and made a note on the yellow pad in his leather-bound notebook. He cocked a questioning eyebrow her way.

Dianne rubbed her hands on her thighs. She cleared her throat and drank some water. "I guess it's because he's avoiding me. I want to have an opportunity to apologize to him. To seek forgiveness, although I don't deserve it. To clear up any misunderstandings. I'm desperately afraid to make any first moves. Oh, hell, I don't know."

Dr. Murphy nodded. "That being said, didn't he make the first move when he spoke to you and told you not to be afraid?"

"Well, I imagine he was looking after his horse. Emperor is a fine animal. Why would Kip want to have anything to do with me? You know what I did. When I left . . ." Dianne stopped talking. Her throat tightened. She fought tears, wiped her eyes with fisted knuckles, and jerked a tissue from the box on the desk.

"I think you're right. You don't know what to do about Kip. I also believe you aren't giving him the benefit of the doubt. He may not be forgiving, but how can you know whether he is or isn't if you fail to make a move of your own?"

"It's just something I can't do. Not yet. Maybe not ever. I've considered returning to New York or maybe another city. I wouldn't be happy but it's easy to disappear there. I know you disagree, but that's how I feel. Maybe getting out and about will help." Dianne lifted her gaze and glanced across the desk in time to catch the look of disapproval she'd known would be on then doctor's face.

"Our time is up." Dr. Murphy stood to usher Dianne out. "I want you to speak to Kip. Just say hello. Enjoy yourself tomorrow. Be carefree. Be indulgent." He accepted Dianne's tentative smile with a squeeze on her arm.

* * * *

The morning's first cup of light, sweet coffee soothed her. She thought more clearly when the day was young and quiet. Dawn edged over the eastern horizon, promising to be a beautiful day.

Dianne sat on the balcony watching gray move to light as the sun rose. The chilly air smelled fresh and clean. She hadn't paid much attention to how polluted New York really was until she came home.

Throwing on some jeans and an oxford shirt, she tossed an apple in her bag, and took off. She'd mapped her stops the night before. The first, in the country club area, seemed promising. She put her hand over her chest, pleased the increase in her heart rate came from excitement rather than anxiety.

She turned the corner and noticed traffic lining the block. A surge of competitive adrenaline raced through Dianne when she parked. She wanted bargains. Gathering her phone, wallet, and keys she practically ran to the door.

"Good morning." Dianne took a bag and informational flyer from a worker.

The newspaper had listed two stained glass lamps. Finding them sat at the top of her personal list. Entering the living room, she saw the lamps bouncing color off the wall like rainbow crystals. Another guest studied them. The young woman ran her hands along the base of a lamp and sighed.

"Aren't they lovely? Can you tell if they're the real thing?" Dianne asked.

"I'm not sure. They're priced like they must be. I can't afford them, but I would love to have one." The woman nodded her hand toward a gathering line of guests. "It appears others want to get a look at these lamps."

Feeling guilty, Dianne motioned for a worker as the young woman walked off. *They're the real thing. Tiffany.* "I would like to purchase these lamps. Can you hold them for me while I finish shopping, and will you wrap this desk lamp for the young woman in the red blouse? I'll pay for it when I check out." Dianne pointed toward the young woman.

Some time later, she made good on that promise. Afterward, pleased with her purchases—lamps, leaded crystal bowls and glasses from Ireland, Christmas decorations, and an antique rolltop desk—Dianne made her way to her car, a smile on her lips. Dr. Murphy would be proud.

* * * *

Caught up in the beauty of the day, Dianne grabbed a burger and headed for a park across from the university. She chose a bench overlooking a clear, small pond. Several ducks took wing, then landed near her. Dianne laughed and threw several French fries into the water. The ducks quacked, flapped their wings, and ruffled their feathers as they fought for the treats. "All right, guys, let me eat a few of these myself."

An uneasy feeling crept into Dianne's consciousness. She looked around but saw nothing out of the ordinary. Chuckling, she leaned back onto the bench and stretched her legs in front of her. But not for long. In a sudden motion, she sat up and rubbed her neck, goose bumps tightening her skin. Someone was watching her.

She stood, looked around once more then gathered her book and purse. Hurrying to her car, she locked the doors and pulled out of the parking space.

Convinced her imagination was in overdrive, she shook off the uncomfortable feeling and allowed the excitement of finding her treasures—foreign, and oh-so-nice—to bubble in her heart.

* * * *

The ringing phone startled her. Who would be calling her on an early Sunday morning? The number looked unfamiliar but had a New York area code. "Hello."

"Good morning, Geneva. Or should I say Dianne since you've returned to the sticks."

She swallowed. Her tongue thickened, making it difficult to speak. "Simon? How did you get this number?"

Had he been watching her at the park yesterday? She shuddered.

The last person she expected to hear from was her ex-husband. Two years had passed since she'd seen or spoken to him. That's when he finally gave in and signed the divorce papers.

Simon laughed. "Jocelyn is so gullible. When my assistant called and said I'd been involved in an accident and he needed to reach you, as my next of kin, she didn't hesitate to give it to him. It was a lie, of course. Actually, I'm here in this godforsaken place."

His perfectly chiseled face would be drawn up in a cruel, condescending smirk. She squeezed her eyes shut against the unwelcome vision.

"Why are you here?" Her voice was shrill. Disdain dripped with every clipped word. The verbal digs would come now, just as they always had.

"You left without telling me. I read about the attack in the paper, for Christ's sake. Nobody ignores me, Dianne. Nobody. Not even my ex-wife. Especially not my ex-wife. People at the office were asking about you. I didn't know and didn't care, but not having answers made me sound like a fool. I've never tolerated being ignored. I won't start now."

Dianne swallowed hard, hoping to quell her churning stomach. "It never occurred to me that I should notify you. Why should I? We're divorced. Answer my question. Why are you here?"

"Where do you live?"

"You are truly crazy. I won't tell you where I live, and I won't meet you. If you have questions, contact my attorney." Dianne ran her fingers through her hair and paced. She didn't trust Simon...and he hadn't told her everything. A click sounded in her ear as he disconnected, leaving her staring at the phone.

* * * *

Simon stood near the kitchen window of the apartment he had leased across from the mansion where Dianne lived. He saw her walk onto her balcony, watched as she leaned over the rail, tugged her hands through her hair, and wiped her eyes. A satisfied chuckle escaped at her actions. He made a cup of coffee and settled into a scuffed leather recliner he had rented. This place lacked the luxuries he was used to, but he didn't expect to be here much longer. His hotel room would be available tomorrow. He'd move about between the two locations as need be. A quick phone call assured him his plans were coming together. *Soon, she'll feel utter shame and sorrow for humiliating me in New York.*

Chapter 5

Dianne arrived at the center ready to ride. She stretched her back and hips, eager to let the upcoming ride take her mind off of Simon's call. Memorized words raced through her mind from her practiced talks with Kip. Be cordial and professional. Talk about the horses, especially Emperor.

Eyes down, she twisted her hair into a messy bun and ran headlong into Kip. "Oh, my God! I'm sorry. Kip, I'm sorry."

His hands gripped her arms. Her heartbeat tripled and jumped from normal to banging so fast she couldn't count the beats—from buried desire to disbelief rather than anxiety. Kip's hand on her arm surprised her. She welcomed the feeling. *I thought I had forgotten the way his touch affected me. Guess not.* She wished he would pull her close enough to feel his heart against hers. Embarrassed at her own thoughts, Dianne placed a hand over her heart and stepped back.

Kip smiled down into her eyes, a welcoming, even forgiving, grin. "Something on your mind, Dianne?"

"Wha–what?" Dianne rubbed her arms. She remembered his gentle but passionate touches and wanted them again. Could she experience that sort of unconditional love again? Did she deserve it?

Kip's hazel eyes softened. "Never mind. Come on...I'll walk you to the stall. Emperor seems to be looking for you."

Emperor and another horse stood saddled in the walkway of the barn. She dug sugar cubes out of her pocket. "I haven't seen that roan before. Is another client going to be riding with me today?"

Kip looked down and cleared his throat. "You've been coming regularly for a while now and you don't seem as nervous. It's time for you to move forward in your therapy. That means going for a real ride."

"A ride? Well, I don't know. Except for safe rides in the arena, I haven't been on a horse in years." Dianne reached up to push loose curls from her face then rolled her shoulders and slumped into herself. Her breath escaped in short gasps.

Kip smiled straight at her, revealing the double dimples she had loved so completely. His soft voice soothed her. "You'll be fine. Riding a horse is kind of like riding a bicycle. Just get on. Besides you used to be rodeo queen and ran barrels faster than anyone in the county. You and Emperor are comfortable together. The roan's my favorite horse, his name's Hunter."

The breath she inhaled felt like scorpions stinging in her chest, but Dianne pressed through the discomfort and allowed him to help her mount. Once Kip had adjusted her stirrups and climbed aboard Hunter, they rode on the bridle trail behind the equestrian center.

Fall flowers colored the pasture—wild red roses, smiling pansies, and grass changing from green to brown. She felt like she was riding into a child's coloring book using a box of sixty-four crayons. The peaceful surrounding spoke to her spirit, and within minutes she completely relaxed. She rode quietly beside Kip until he challenged her with a grin and a wink.

Her forehead wrinkled, not sure what he meant. "What?"

"Ready? Let's go!" Kip urged Hunter into a lope. He looked back, daring Dianne. "Coming?"

Dianne gave Emperor a kick, urging him into a gallop. She passed Kip and didn't want to stop. The challenge of a race took over all sense. Without a second thought, she laughed and stretched low over Emperor's neck. The sensation of absolute freedom coursed through her body and left through the reins she held. Her horse instinctively stretched out and ran faster. "Run, Emperor, run until you want to stop."

Kip pulled back on the reins to slow his horse. Dianne needed the gallop. He hoped she would leave some of her demons behind. Watching her ride with such abandon filled his heart. Difficult to believe he might still be in love with her after all these years. *Is it love or just relief that she's improving? Will she break my heart again? Do I want to take that risk?*

The sting of betrayal returned, along with guarded trust. The sound of her laughter flew back to him. Lord help him, she was more beautiful than ever. Strawberry-blonde hair had escaped its flimsy confines and trailed behind her like a silken curtain. Over the years he had detached from her. Time after time. *I'll just treat her like any other client. Working with her is part of the job.*

Ricochet's words and warnings echoed through his heart and mind. He'd promised his friend he would talk to Dianne and keep an open mind without dwelling on the past. Thing was, he'd never stopped living in the past as far as Dianne Raborn was concerned.

An hour later, the two stood in the barn grooming the horses.

"Emperor, my healer, you are one magnificent animal. How I wish you were mine."

Dianne's cheeks flushed with excitement and her eyes gleamed with pride. When she turned toward him, his heart dropped to his gut and his knees threatened to give out on him. *I wonder how she'll feel when she learns that Emperor is her horse.* For an instant their eyes locked, lips parted, and arms lifted toward one another before falling to their sides.

Dianne smiled. "Thank you for this day. I will never forget it."

"Part of the job." Kip spit the words out, regretting them immediately. The look on Dianne's face—crushed and saddened—forced him to eat those words.

She stepped away as he drew near. Kip hesitated to reach for her. "I'm sorry. I didn't intend to sound that way. Have you had any lemon pie since you got back?"

"Pie? What does that have to do with anything?" Dianne wiped her eyes.

He touched her shoulder. "Would you like to have some pie and coffee before you head home? I go at least once a week. Wanna meet me at the old diner?"

Dianne nodded.

* * * *

What in hell am I doing? Dianne questioned her too-quick agreement as she climbed into the booth opposite Kip.

Stilted silence and tentative smiles filled the space until they reached for the tabletop jukebox at the same time.

Dianne chuckled low in her throat. "Yeah, but I always had better taste in music than you."

The waitress came to the table and asked for their order. "We'll have a piece of lemon and one of chocolate."

Teasing and laughter at stupid things like the weather and movies relaxed them.

The waitress brought their pie. "Here you go. Enjoy."

Dianne fumbled with her napkin before taking a bite. "Oh, my gracious. This is so good. I haven't had anything like this in forever."

"Don't they have pie in New York? Lemon pie used to be your favorite. Want some music?" He flipped through the juke box.

"We had pie, generally some kind of flat ice box recipe. Not made with real crust and four inches of meringue." She licked her lips.

Elvis Presley's unique voice and a visual of him shaking his hips filled their space singing 'All Shook Up'. "Remember how we put all of our quarters in this crazy machine?"

"Yeah, I do." Dianne finished off her pie and scraped the plate with her fork. "Is your chocolate good?"

"Wanna bite?" Kip speared a piece of pie and reached across the table, offering it to her.

She steadied the fork in his hand and took a large, unladylike bite. "Very tasty." The dangerous gleam in Kip's eyes made her nervous. He ran his fingers along his lips which still looked soft and sensual. Just thinking about his kisses made her knees shake beneath the table. She put her hands on them to stop the trembling.

"Uh, Dianne, you have meringue and chocolate on your chin." He grinned.

Heat rose in her face. She jerked the napkin from her lap and wiped her mouth. "Better?"

He chuckled and nodded. "How do you like coming to the center? I know it was hard on you at first."

"I like it now, but yeah, at first it caused nothing but anxiety. I've met a few of the other clients. Everyone loves the horses. I do wonder about children, though. The brochure mentioned therapy for kids. I haven't seen any around. What about that?"

"Have you noticed the big barn to the west?"

Dianne nodded.

"That's the barn the kids go to. They're the most amazing little people. When we first opened, we mostly had relatively healthy Special Olympics kids who benefitted from being near the horses. Now, we have some really sick guys. One little boy we call Chief is blind and deaf. He'll never walk or talk or eat like we do. But, my God, when he shows up in his special wheelchair, his horse—an arthritic Welsh pony named Molly—greets him with a whinny. I swear he hears her. He kicks his legs and makes noises. They have a bond." Kip cleared his throat and blinked then wiped his eyes with his thumbs.

Kip crying? Never in a million years. Dianne reached across the table and squeezed his hand. "That's amazing."

"The majority of the horses over there are smaller breeds. All of them are gentle and trained to be patient. You put one of those kids on the back of the horse and give them the reins, and even though you're holding a lead line, they feel as if they're in control. For a few minutes, they feel normal. One of my favorite little girls is a blue-eyed blonde who is lost inside herself. Nobody knows why. She's paired with a miniature horse just her size. The leader of the pack over there is a stubborn, grey-muzzled old burro named Padre who truly acts like the protective Papa of the kids and horses."

"Could I go over there one of these days?"

"Sure, but I have to check on confidentiality issues first. Listen, I need to get back to the ranch. You ready to leave?" He dropped some bills on top of the check the waitress had left.

Dianne gathered her purse and phone. "Yeah. Thank you for the pie. It was wonderful."

Kip escorted Dianne to her car. He whistled long and low when she unlocked the red luxury vehicle. "Nice ride."

"Thanks. I didn't have a car in New York, so I had to get one when I left. My friend, Jocelyn, said this is a good model. The salesman may have taken advantage of my ignorance, but I do like it." She babbled, and embarrassing tears sprang to life. Suddenly she was sad. Not anxious, just melancholy. Life had passed her by while she chased what she believed was her own definition of success.

"Damn. What's wrong? Did I do something?" Kip pulled her to him, rocked her, and whispered in her ear that he was confused, and he knew the girl he loved was still in there.

Leaning into his chest, Dianne let go and cried. Not tears of frustration or fear, but of deep regret. She pulled away, wiped her eyes with the back of her hand, and struggled to speak. "I am sorry, Kip. For everything. Now that I've come home I have, I want, to make amends. You have been kinder than I deserve."

"I could never be mean to you. I'll always care for you, and I'll be there the next time you come to see Emperor." Kip kissed her lightly on the forehead.

Dianne rubbed her hand over the wet spot on his shirt. "Sorry about your shirt. I think what I need right now is a bath and a mindless movie."

He touched her lips, then turned, leaving her standing beside the car.

Fresh tears sprang into her eyes. They would eventually have to talk things out. The time for the confrontation she dreaded would happen soon. She was afraid, not sure if she had broken his heart again or if it had started to thaw. She carried the shattered shards of the past in her heart and soul. She believed they both still held their young love in their hearts. For a woman used to fighting for the rights of others, she didn't believe in herself anymore. But she would.

Back home, she picked up a soda, a lap blanket, and a book by one of her favorite authors, then headed to the basement. Coming down here had become a habit not long after she returned to Wichita Falls. Despite the mustiness, comfort eased through her. She opened the novel and let herself be swept away from the worries of her life…at least for the moment.

Chapter 6

"Here we are. Home. I'm so relieved to have you here." Dianne reached across the seat and squeezed her best friend's hand.

"This is where you live?" Jocelyn's wide gaze took in Dianna's place. "You said it was big, but…sweetie, you didn't say it was a mansion."

Dianne laughed and helped Jocelyn with her luggage. "I don't live in the whole thing. I have a suite on the second floor. Careful on the stairs. They can be tricky."

She pointed to the door of her suite but stopped to look over the mezzanine railing into the foyer and formal living room. "Isn't it beautiful? I'm loving it here. This is my favorite view because I can see the carved images on the first-floor fireplace and the pool through the stained glass doors."

Joining her, Jocelyn leaned over the railing and sighed. "Are those faces on the fireplace mythological gods?"

"Yeah, it's Italian marble." Dianne moved to the door and unlocked her suite. She stood back with her arms crossed as Jocelyn took in the cream-colored love seats flanking a marble fireplace and two burgundy wing chairs facing it.

"It's enormous and it suits you. Only you could take one large room and turn it into a kitchen, living room, and office."

"I wouldn't say that, but I feel safe here."

Jocelyn walked toward the floor-to-ceiling windows on each side of a rolltop desk. "What's outside?"

"The side yard and beyond that, the highway. When the place was completed in 1926, nothing but pasture stretched out for miles. Now there's s a freeway. Come on, let me show you the bedroom and bathroom. You can store your things in there. Let's have some wine."

Jocelyn swirled the pink liquid, sending colorful prisms from the crystal glass. She took a sip then pulled a jeweled clip from her dark hair. "God, I'm tired. It's a long way from San Francisco to Texas when you have layovers. Especially after a full day of work. Now tell me about Kip."

"You asked about the equestrian center earlier. I enjoy going but I get so nervous around Kip. Emperor, my horse, is trusting and accepting. I groom him every time I go. It's then that I can relax enough to think. I talk to him, and I believe he understands every word. Kip comes around sometimes, mostly to check on the horses. I don't see him every time I go."

"I remember back in college you said Kip saved you. That was important. Maybe that's reason you get so nervous."

Dianne kicked off her shoes and pulled a lap blanket over her knees. Memories of Kip moved through her mind. "You're probably right. I was the target of bullies. Anger, shame about my dad, and a general lack of self-confidence ruled my life. Kip stood up for me. He told the bullies to back off. That was all it took. He saved me once and it seems life is putting me in the direct path of needing to be saved again. We started dating and the rest is history."

"You know, seeing him might remind you of the bad times and the good ones." Jocelyn yawned and sipped her wine. She closed her eyes and rested against the sofa pillows.

"That makes sense. But the other thing it does is resurrect the guilt I felt, and still feel, for leaving. We can talk tomorrow. Come on, let's go to bed. I have an appointment at the equestrian center tomorrow. Besides, you look like hell." Dianne stood, glass in hand, took her friend's empty one, and carried them both to the galley kitchen.

* * * *

Dianne couldn't sleep. She got up and settled in a chair, careful not to wake Jocelyn. Vivid images of her father stumbling into the house after a night of drinking and drugging rose in her mind, and she could almost hear her mother's frantic voice insisting she go to her room and lock the door. She shut her eyes when memories assaulted her. They seemed so real, she shuddered and pulled the blanket over her shoulders, just like she did when she was a kid. Memory-sounds assaulted her senses—angry curses, begging, glass breaking, and sirens screaming down the street. She hold her breath and put her hands over her ears. Her father was arrested that night. Again. He didn't come back that time.

Like most small towns, Waurika spread news like a prairie wildfire—especially news that could be considered juicy. The next morning at school, the taunting and bullying escalated just like she expected. A girl named Anne possessed a shrill voice with a contempt that could cut through marble.

The angst Dianne managed to smother as a teenager roared back to life with the memories. Guilt had consumed her then, because she was relieved her father was gone.

After he was thrown in jail, then sent to state prison, her mother blossomed. She got a job at the bank and bought new clothes for Dianne and herself. *I had a yellow dress I loved. The two of us were happy.* Her breath caught on a strangled sob. *But then lung cancer came calling, and took mom's life just before high school graduation. I was alone, an orphan with a questionable future ahead of me. Truly, I only wanted Kip.*

Dianne's heart broke again. She fought to control the shaky sobs building in her chest. Gaining control of herself, she got up, made a mug of hot chocolate, and picked up her laptop. A few minutes of mindless browsing would settle her down and numb her imagination.

Tomorrow Jocelyn and I will just enjoy the day.

* * * *

Dianne showered, twisted a towel around her head, and went in search of her guest. She found Jocelyn sitting cross-legged on the floor, leaning against the sofa. Open yearbooks covered the floor around her.

"Interesting, aren't they? Especially after fifteen years." Dianne claimed the spot beside her.

"I found several photos I want to ask you about. Especially this one." Jocelyn pointed to an image.

Dianne glanced over to see which one captured Joycelyn's curiosity. "Oh. That one. I was fifteen and angry at the world. I glared at the photographer and his stupid efforts to get me to smile. That one was before I knew Kip."

"And these. In all three books you and Kip received several honors. Cutest couple three years in a row. Honor societies. You were a rodeo queen and voted most likely to succeed. Why didn't you ever tell me these things?"

Dianne shrugged. "'These things' were part of my past—a past I didn't like thinking about. One I was running from, trying to forget. Guilt and regret burdened me almost every waking moment, and often in the night, at first. Those feelings lessened while you and I shared a college dorm room. I guess because I had you—a friend who accepted me for just being me—is the reason I never said anything.

"Plus, I had to study all the time to stay on top of things and maintain my scholarship. I never felt worthy of any of the accolades in high school. Kip earned and deserved them all. I always assumed I received them because of him. His parents worked for the biggest ranch in the area. Everyone knew and respected his family. We moved to Oklahoma the summer between junior high and high school. My family was never accepted because of my dad." Dianne shuddered.

Jocelyn shifted to look directly at Dianne. "Did Kip know how you felt?"

"I don't know. I don't think so. He loved me without condition, he taught me about love. I left because I wanted out of that town. When I saw him with that cheerleader, leaving seemed to be the best thing to do. I hoped my leaving would give him an opportunity to find someone more deserving. So, I took the scholarship. I broke his heart and mine, and didn't have the courage to tell him why." Dianne's eyes filled with tears, but she didn't allow them to fall. She leaned back as limp as if her body lost all muscle control, exhaled, and wiped her hands on her thighs.

"I think it's time for you to move forward."

"You're right, of course. The mind is a curious thing. I always feel off kilter, yet I believe I'm where I'm supposed to be. Including with Kip. He has his life. I'm building a new one. Still not sure if I'll stay here permanently but I feel better about the move." Dianne touched the small galloping horse charm dangling from a gold chain around her neck, soothed by the memory of when he gave it to her. "Time to get dressed. We have an appointment to keep."

They left the house in a rush and picked up breakfast sandwiches from McDonald's. "I think you're in for a real treat today."

Dianne pulled into the parking lot of the Horses of Hope Equestrian Center. She pointed to a truck and trailer parked at the far end. "That's Kip's rig. He's here."

"Good. I get to meet him. I hope. You know I've never been near a horse, right?"

"Yeah. You'll be fine." Dianne picked up her purse and prowled to the bottom of it. She brought out a prescription bottle and swallowed a pill with a slurp of coffee.

"What is that?"

"My medication for anxiety. I always need one before I get to the center. It helps relieve the threat of panic attacks."

Jocelyn's brow wrinkled. "Is that medicine a problem? You always swore you would never take any kind of addictive drugs, even with a prescription, because of your dad."

Dianne's insides tightened with irritation. She fought to keep the annoyance from showing on her face or in her body language when she climbed out of the car. *Seriously? Jocelyn concerned over anxiety meds? If she'd been through what I have, she might be more understanding.* Still, Jocelyn cared about her. The expression on her friend's face left no question about that as she too, got out of the car. "It's not a problem. I just don't want to have a panic attack. Especially if Kip is around. I'm learning to control the anxiety instead of the other way around."

Dianne pushed the door to the center open. Jocelyn followed her inside and stumbled over the threshold when the overhead cowbell rang.

Beth manned the desk, stuffing envelopes. "Good morning, Dianne. Here, let me give you one of these invitations to save a stamp."

Dianne put the letter in her pocket and looped an arm around Jocelyn's shoulder. "Beth, let me introduce you to my dear friend from San Francisco. This is Jocelyn Hartford. Jocelyn, this is Beth Kelso. Beth is the secretary and energy source for the center."

Jocelyn reached to take Beth's hand.

Beth lurched out of her chair, sending it rolling behind her. She enfolded Jocelyn in a bear hug. "Hi! I'm so happy to meet you. You're certainly welcome here. How long will you be visiting? You know, I've never been to San Francisco. I've never even been to California. I bet it's nice."

Jocelyn looked at Dianne with wide eyes as Beth chattered on without taking a single breath.

Dianne shrugged and grinned.

"I'm not sure how long I'll be here, Beth. I always heard Texans talk slowly. You surely don't. San Francisco is a lovely city and very diverse. Maybe you can visit one day. Feel free to get my numbers from Dianne."

"Do you know if Emperor is ready?" Dianne asked and winked at Jocelyn.

Beth nodded. "Kip's out there. We're working on organizing the round-up. I left about midnight. He was still here."

Dianne arched her brow in curiosity. "Really?" Ignoring the smug look on Beth's face, she walked to the barn with Jocelyn beside her. Her heart rate increased. Not in panic, but excitement and anticipation. She couldn't pretend how important seeing Kip was to her.

She laughed when Jocelyn made a guttural noise in her throat and covered her nose and mouth with her hand. "My God, what is that smell?"

Several horses held their heads over the stall gates with their ears forward. Some nickered. Others pranced in place and lifted their head as though greeting the ladies. "That, my friend, is the smell of horse flesh, manure, and hay. I like it better than the most expensive perfume from Paris."

Jocelyn stood so still she looked like a robot.

Dianne stopped at a stall, rubbed the horse's face, and scratched his ears before pulling some sugar cubes from her pocket "Good morning, Big Boy. I have someone I want you to meet."

She gave Jocelyn two treats and taught her to hold her hand flat to give it to Emperor. "Keep your palm flat so he can't bite you."

Jocelyn stepped back and stuffed her hands in her pockets. "No freaking way. Not if he bites."

"He doesn't bite. It's just hard for a horse to get something from your hand if it isn't flat. Go on give him a pat on the neck and his treat. He'll love you forever."

After one step forward and two back, Jocelyn made it to the stall gate. She touched Emperor's neck with the tips of her finger. He nickered and stretched his head over the gate trying to reach the sweet treat in her hand. When he snorted, she gasped and stepped back. "You give it to him. He doesn't like me."

"That's nuts. He likes you. You just don't know how to read horse body language."

"Horses have body language?"

Dianne nodded and watched as Jocelyn gathered her courage and held out the treat once more. She grinned at the awe on her friend's face when Emperor gobbled it up.

Joycelyn wiped her hand on her pants. "I didn't know his nose would feel like velvet."

Laughter rumbled from the next stall. Dianne peeked around to find Kip sitting in the corner. He stood, unfolding to his full height, stretched his back, and combed his unruly hair with his fingers before putting on his hat. He waltzed out of the corner grinning like a kid in trouble. "Mornin', Dianne. Who's your friend?"

Oh, damn. "Kip Mahan, this is my friend Jocelyn Hartford." The familiar rise of heat crawled up her face. As red as a clown's rubber nose, she thought with disgust. *Why does being near him make my body act up?*

Kip smiled, tipped his hat, and reached to shake Jocelyn's hand. "Nice to meet you. Haven't been around horses much, have you?"

"No. I haven't. This is my first time to touch one. I'm a big-city girl." Jocelyn lifted her eyebrow toward Dianne.

Dianne rested against a stall as Kip charmed her friend. Even back in high school he had the ability to flutter hearts. Her memories burst forth and drowned out his and Joycelyn's conversation which buzzed like a honeybee in the background.

The first time she and Kip went riding, she had never been on a horse. Her mount was an old trail horse with a swaying, sleepy gait. Before the ride finished and the horses were back in the corral she'd been hooked. She told Kip she wanted to learn to really ride. He borrowed a ranch horse for her. She practiced as much as possible and started winning a few play-day events. A few weeks before her sixteenth birthday Kip gave her a pretty palomino mare. She called her Honeybee. They became a team to be reckoned with.

Emperor nickered, forcing her to shake the cobwebs of memories and join the others. "You ready to ride?"

She led the horse out of the stall, saddled him, and stopped in front of Kip and Jocelyn. "I'm heading out to the round ring. You joining me?"

Jocelyn grimaced. "I guess. Ready as I'll ever be."

Laughing, Dianne mounted and trotted to the ring covered in sand.

Within moments her horse had been through the expected gait changes—walking, trotting, and cantering. The round arena offered a glimpse of Jocelyn and Kip every few seconds. Kip stood with one booted foot on the bottom rail of the fence. Jocelyn peered through the rails smiling and waving.

Careful to keep her heels down and back straight, Dianne relaxed. With a soft smile and loose reins, she let Emperor take the lead. Kip pointed to her and said something to Jocelyn.

Kip put two fingers in his mouth and whistled. "Show us a fast cloverleaf?"

"Are you nuts?" What the hell is he thinking? She hadn't done that in years! Her heart hammered, but Dianne gripped the reins tighter and settled her boots in the stirrups. Pulling back on the reins until Emperor stopped. She whispered a prayer and kicked him into a full gallop, guiding him around the barrels in the center of the ring. She whooped and rode over to Kip, skidding to a stop. "Oh, my God. My God! I did it, Kip."

She jumped down. Her feet barely touched the ground before Kip scooped her into his arms and hugged her to him. He looked down at her, his gaze dropped to her mouth. For a moment she thought he was going to kiss her. She held her breath and waited. His warm body pressed to hers weakened her knees. Kip blinked, then set her away from him.

Dianne smothered her disappointment.

"What did she do?" Jocelyn asked.

"She did a perfect cloverleaf pattern on a horse that's never run one. He's a natural." Kip rubbed Emperor's nose.

Dianne doubled over and inhaled a few deep breaths. Joy and pride bloomed in her heart. She laughed. "He's spectacular."

"He sure is. Great ride, Dianne." Kip's voice rang with admiration.

Dianne crossed her arms over her chest, trying to hold her heart in place. She had hoped he would kiss her. She'd seen the shadow cross his face and knew the pain she'd inflicted fifteen years ago still ran deep. Of course, he'd be thrilled his horse was a natural. "Thank you."

"Ladies, I better get to work. Have a good day."

Dianne couldn't pull her eyes away from the sight of him walking away.

Chapter 7

A few hours later, Dianne had shown Jocelyn everything she wanted her to see at the center and around town. She remembered the letter Beth had given her and pulled it out of her pocket, then let out a low whistle. "I, and a guest, have been invited to a shindig at the 3G. It's two days away and includes several rodeo events that include roping, sorting calves, branding, vaccinating, and castrating. Lots of food and a dance after dark. It's a full workday on the ranch."

Jocelyn shuddered. "Castrating? Sounds…barbaric. Does it hurt the cows?" She sighed. "I'll try to go with the flow. The only thing you said that I liked was food and dancing."

"First of all, cows don't get castrated. Bull calves do. This is one business where females are more important than males. Steers—that's castrated calves—usually end up on a dinner plate. Female calves—you've heard of heifers—are valued for their ability to reproduce. You'll experience things you've never seen and probably wouldn't want to see again. I want to go. Kip will be there as well as some old friends. I haven't seen anyone else since I got back."

Her stomach churned at the thought of what kind of reception she might receive. "To be honest, I'm afraid they might not want me around since I hurt Kip so badly."

Jocelyn hesitated. "I'm going to say two things. Your former friends may not accept you back into their fold. Times have changed. They have new lives, just as you do. You can't dwell on it at all. I think it's time you and Kip had a real heart-to-heart talk. The chemistry between you two threatened to burn that barn down today. This event may provide that chance. How long until you have to RSVP?"

"Tomorrow. Being around Kip just sends my emotions on a roller-coaster ride. Hope. Nerves. Feeling inadequate and undeserving. I don't know if I'm even worthy of a second chance. But I want one." Her hands shook. She wiped them on her jeans and lifted her gaze to her friend.

"I'll be with you. You'll see, time will melt away." Jocelyn stepped closer and embraced Dianne.

She shoved her fingers through her hair, undoing the braid. "What if Kip doesn't know Beth gave me an invitation? You saw how he shut himself down."

"Listen, I know the mugging stole your confidence. Simon stole part of it. But, damn, I've never known you to be this nerve wracked. Besides, didn't you see the list of people being invited? It was initialed by both Kip and Beth. He knows. He wants you there."

Dianne pulled the pill she had taken from her purse out of her front pocket and swallowed it. She allowed Jocelyn to take her hand.

"How often are you taking these things? I'm worried. Is it a problem? Listen, I would love to go to this cowboy thing but if it's going to set you back, we shouldn't do it."

"It's not a problem. Don't worry. How should we spend the rest of the day?"

"Shopping. I'm positive I don't have anything appropriate for this hoe-down."

* * * *

The rich earthy scents of leather, pungent liniment, and grain greeted them when they entered the western wear, tack, and equestrian supply store. Dianne inhaled deeply. "Smell that? It's new leather."

"It's nice, but not as nice as handbags from Milan." Jocelyn stood on tiptoes looking for the clothing department.

Dianne moved straight to a saddle display. She rubbed her hand over the smooth leather of the seat and traced the tooling on the stirrup skirts. With a sigh, she moved away and crossed to the women's section with Jocelyn. "I love that saddle. Come on, let's look at shirts first."

"Stop. Wait." Jocelyn took Dianne's hand and pulled her to a rack of vests. With one hand, she held up a black suede one with fringe on the hem. In the other she raised one of cowhide.

"Well, they're western. I think. Stereotypical, but cute."

Jocelyn stood in front of a mirror. One by one, she pulled the vests on, twirled, and danced. "I want them. What do you think? Will they work?"

"I think we should find shirts first, but I know you. Get the vests. Don't forget Wranglers and boots."

"What are Wranglers?"

Dianne couldn't hold back the guffaw that erupted from her. "Jeans, it's a brand of jeans. Just don't get pink boots. Beth will have those."

An hour later they'd completed their shopping. "What were you thinking, Joc? Three shirts, two vests, two pairs of jeans, a skirt, two pairs of boots, and socks. Overkill, don't you think?"

"Maybe, but I loved it. I haven't had this much fun in ages. Plus, I looked adorable. Tomorrow I'll wear the cowhide vest in the day and dazzle everyone with the fringed one at the dance. Look who's talking, you bought your fair share."

Dianne threw her head back and laughed. Letting go and having fun felt good. She had forgotten. She made a promise to find ways to laugh in the future.

"What are you laughing at?"

"I never in a million years imagined I would see you excited about western wear. It's an extreme…deviation…from your usual designer clothes."

Jocelyn shrugged. "When in Rome and all that."

Dianne's heart felt light as they headed home in the evening dusk. This was a day she would cherish until she sat rocking on the porch drinking tea. What a blessing to have such a devoted and understanding friend. She slipped her chin to her chest and uttered a private prayer of thanksgiving.

Chapter 8

"Rise and shine, Cowgirl." Dianne put a mug of hot coffee on the bedside table and sang out the greeting to her friend.

Jocelyn's soft snoring stopped. She lifted her head, looked to the window, and groaned. "What time is it? The sun isn't all the way up."

"Come on, no sleeping in around here."

Jocelyn sat up, pushed the curtain of tangled hair out of her face, and took the coffee. "What's the hurry?"

"Ranches start early, especially on round-up days. I haven't been to one in years, and I don't want to miss a thing. Time to go, get up. Make sure you take a change of clothes for the dance."

Jocelyn grumbled and gulped her coffee as if it was a lifeline. She rolled over and put her feet on the floor. "Maybe a shower will wake me up. Something has to at this godforsaken hour."

Dianne chuckled and watched her stumble to the bathroom. She took the invitation letter from her purse and caressed Kip's name embossed on it. This day promised to be busy, tiring, and exhilarating. Would Kip let her help herd the calves into the corral? Closing her eyes, she retrieved happy memories of horses whinnying, cows and calves bawling, cowboys shouting, and lassoes snapping. She winced when she recalled the acrid smell of burning hair and flesh when the calves were branded. Kip used to tease her when she backed away and fought tears when the calves were separated from their mothers.

Dianne looked up when Jocelyn returned to the room. "You look great. That vest was a good choice but you're going to regret the white shirt before the day is done. No one will notice, though, because you look as leggy as a colt in those boots and jeans."

"Hush. Let's go before I chicken out. However, the dance sounds intriguing. I'm looking forward to that."

Dianne loaded the car while Jocelyn prepared two travel mugs of coffee. She took a few deep breaths, determined to halt the rising anxiety building in her core. *Nothing* could ruin her mood today.

As they drove, Dianne pointed to a gravel-topped road leading to a large log home on the bluff. "That's the ranch, but I want to show you where I grew up before we go to the round-up. Waurika, small town U.S.A."

"It's beautiful out here. Desolate even. Is the sky always this blue?" Jocelyn looked in every direction, including standing to see everything through the sunroof.

"Nothing like New York or San Francisco to be sure. No pollution. All of this seemed bigger when I was a kid. Most of us wanted nothing more than to get out of town. I was one of them. I thought. Kip never wanted to leave. Now, I'm back and I want nothing more than the peace." Dianne puffed out her cheeks and turned onto the almost-deserted Main Street with no traffic lights or stop signs along its length.

"This bricked street has always been one of my favorite parts of town. It seemed so quaint. I loved, still love, the rumble of tires against it. Things weren't as rundown when I was a kid. Almost every store was open. That drug store was always the busiest place after school. Kids rushed to get there first and claim stools at the counter. I loved the strawberry shakes. Kip always ordered a cherry Coke and Teresa got a vanilla-cream Dr. Pepper.

"They had two racks of comic books. I think Mr. Zimmerman made sure the racks squeaked with every turn. You could get about anything there. Medicine, kitchen supplies, perfume, make-up, some groceries, toys, and seasonal things. I loved this place. I'm glad it's still open, but it isn't the same."

"I can see why things in disrepair makes you sad."

"Yeah, they do. Nowadays, I yearn for the quiet life I once hated. But, then again, I don't know if I'm heading toward a new life or falling backward into a pit of my own making." Dianne knuckled away tears.

"Do you wish you had stayed in New York, now that Kip is back in your life?"

"I don't know. I wouldn't change my experience in New York or the education we received. But, yes, I do have regrets. Plenty. I've given a great deal of thought as to what my life would have been like if I had stayed. I've even thought about going back before I hurt anyone again."

"I don't think there's a chance you might hurt Kip again. Besides, why would you even think about going back to New York? Simon is there. The mugger is there. You never really liked the city. If you run before you find out where this all leads, you'll live with regret and sorrow."

"New York's a big place. Besides, Simon is actually here."

"What the hell do you mean, 'here'? Simon's *here*…as in this town?" Jocelyn shook her head.

Dianne nodded. "He called me. Said you'd given him my number."

"That's crazy. Nuts. You know I would never do that, right?"

"I know. You were manipulated into giving it to one of his minions."

Jocelyn slapped her palm against her forehead. "Oh, God, I'm so sorry! What did he say?"

"Just a veiled threat. He's bluffing…at least, I hope he is." Dianne shrugged, determined to put Simon out of her mind. She turned back onto the highway and headed to the ranch.

She followed hand-written signs and primary-colored banners to designated parking for the 3G round-up. Wind gusts forced the flags to flip and flop on the rope. Dianne pulled in next to a truck and rested against the head rest. Her hands shook despite the white-knuckled grip on the steering wheel. Concentrating on her breathing, she took a brown bottle of pills from her tote bag and tossed one back then frowned at the questioning look Jocelyn sent her way. "It's just my anxiety medicine. Are you ready for this?"

"Looks like I should be asking you that question. We can go back if you need to. I'm becoming concerned about how many of those pills you're taking."

"I want to stay. About the pills, I don't take more than is prescribed and I often go without any at all. I don't have a problem." Dianne tucked stray strands of hair behind her ears and rubbed her eyes with her fingertips to make sure her make-up didn't smear.

Jocelyn lifted her eyebrows then released the seat belt. "I'm the one who should be panicked. By the way, don't let negative debates set up housekeeping in your head about what you should or shouldn't do and impact what Kip is trying to do for you. Open your eyes. Just open your eyes."

Dianne smiled and pulled on a western hat. "Today is going to be all about seeing old friends, working a round-up, and forgetting my problems. I can do this."

They walked to the registration table manned by Beth. Dianne shoved her flattened hand into the waistband of her jeans and tucked her denim shirt in a bit snugger. Confidence pushed doubt aside for one exhilarating moment.

Beth bounced out of her chair and rounded the table to greet them. She sparkled from her sequined hatband to the silver tips on her boots. Even her denim blouse flashed with well-placed sequins.

"Good morning! I'm glad you came. You'll enjoy the day. If you need anything let me know."

"Do you know what Kip has in store for me?" Dianne asked.

"He wants you in the corral to help sort the cows and calves. First, go have a big breakfast. You'll need your energy." She turned and pointed to the food tent and waved to others.

They had almost reached the tent when a voice stopped them. "Dianne. Dianne Raborn? Goodness, it is you! You look wonderful."

A woman ran toward her waving her hand and carrying a baby. Dianne frowned. Questions flooded her mind. Hints of recognition moved among her memories. Then she knew. "Teresa. It's good to see you. You're radiant."

Teresa loosened the baby's fist from her hair and reached to pull a waist length braid over her shoulder. "Welcome home."

The hug Dianne received radiated welcome. No guilt or anger, only love and the sticky fingers of a baby holding a well-gummed cookie. She rocked back cupping Teresa's cheek in one hand. Her eyes filled with happy, relieved tears, unlike those shed in the past few years borne of loneliness, frustration, and panic. "Thanks. Did your mother tell you I saw her? And who is this pretty little girl?"

Teresa kissed the baby on the forehead. "Mom told me. I've wanted to get in touch, but the kids keep me running in circles. This is little Hannah. She's our baby. We have two more, six- year-old Stoney and three-year-old Elizabeth. I married Josh Howard when we finished college."

"I'm sorry I didn't contact you before or after I left. I hope you'll forgive me. One day soon we can talk about everything. Will you join us for breakfast? This is my friend Jocelyn Hartford; she's visiting from San Francisco. Jocelyn, this is Teresa Howard."

The two women shook hands, and Dianne moved between her two friends encircling each with an arm. She enjoyed the feelings overriding any hint of anxiety, kind of like a department store comforter wrapped around a too-short wool blanket. Teresa's open acceptance warmed her heart and chipped away another doubt. She would earn forgiveness.

Spurs jingled and chaps squeaked. She knew without turning Kip and someone else walked up behind them. The women turned at the same time. Baby Hannah squealed and held out her arms. Her four teeth sparkled. "Da-Da."

Dianne smiled when Josh took his daughter in his arms. She never imagined he would be so besotted by a pair of blue eyes and chubby cheeks beneath a bald head. "It's good to see you, Josh. You look like a natural holding that baby."

"This little girl has me wrapped around her tiny finger. That's a sure thing."

"I can tell." Dianne looked past Josh to Kip. His eyes crinkled at the corners when he sent her a lopsided grin. It would be easy to fall into his muscled arms and let the world fade away. She knew she would feel secure. Heat rose from the depths of her belly to her face. She swallowed against the dryness in her throat. "Are you here to make us work? Beth said you wanted me in the corral."

"Yep, but first a real cowboy breakfast. It's hard work, remember? Eat a big breakfast because you'll be in the saddle for hours."

"I remember."

The small group walked to the chow tent.

Dianne took a steaming cup from a fresh-faced caterer. She moaned when she took the first sip. Funny how coffee tastes better from a blue tin cup. Holding the mug in both hands for warmth she raised it to her lips and inhaled, savoring the strong, bold aroma. She listened to the chatter, sounds of cattle milling and lowing, horses nickering, and the snap of lassoes cutting through the morning air. Her stomach lurched when the acrid scent of a wood fire in the center of the corral triggered unpleasant memories of branding calves.

Several horses tied to a rope picket line varied in their reaction to the day. The younger ones pulled on their reins and pawed the ground. The more experienced ones relaxed with their heads down and eyes closed. Despite her success in the business world and the too-many to count accolades and awards she earned, nothing felt as good as these anxiety free moments promising a new life in a different direction. She sighed and took a contented breath.

Two plates piled high with biscuits, cream gravy, bacon, sausage, scrambled eggs, hashbrowns, and pancakes slid down the trestle table to Dianne and Jocelyn. She reached for the flatware and salt then dug in with a raging appetite. "This is the best. Nothing like fresh air and cool mornings to make me hungry. What do you think, J.?"

Jocelyn shook her head. "I've never seen so much food on one plate in my life. I don't know what some of these things are. I usually just have yogurt if anything at all."

Kip wedged himself between Dianne and Jocelyn, his plate and mouth full. He swallowed. "What do you think? The bacon and sausage came from my own hog and the eggs are from my chickens. Jocelyn, have you ever seen a hog get butchered?"

Dianne covered her mouth to keep from laughing when Jocelyn paled and choked. She pounded her on the back. "Sorry. It was funny."

Kip held a piece of bacon. "Here you go, Dianne. I remember you like it crisp."

Dianne took the offering. Her eyes locked on Kip's. Leaning in to kiss him would be the simplest, most natural next move. She turned her gaze away before she did exactly that. What kind of fool was she? Ready and willing to make a spectacle of herself—and in front of a crowd of people.

Kip stuffed a piece of sausage in the middle of a biscuit and stood to leave the table. He edged closer and whispered in Dianne's ear. "When you're done, please join me at the house. I want to show you something."

Dianne couldn't speak. Her stomach lurched and she pretended to wipe her hands on the napkin. She couldn't imagine what he wanted. Why would he want her at his house? "Sure, I'm finished now."

"I'll catch up with you later." The wicked gleam in Jocelyn's eyes said a whole lot more than the simple statement implied

Chapter 9

Dianne followed Kip in silence. The walk wasn't long, only about a hundred yards that felt like a thousand and seemed to take forever. As they approached the two-story ranch house she stopped in her tracks. The railing of the wrap-around porch and the outdoor furniture was almost an exact testament to a dream she and Kip had shared. A leaded glass door glimmered as light pierced through the panes, only to bounce off jewel-toned prisms. Rocking chairs and a cushioned swing beckoned. Red geraniums in moss-lined baskets held court beneath each window, and jasmine climbed a trellis. The scene before her smelled like romance.

"I don't know what to say. Everything is breathtaking. Even...stunning, Kip. You've done well."

"Thanks." He held the door open and motioned her inside.

She walked through the heavy door. Questions screamed in her head. Why was she here? What did he want? Would this lead to a reconciliation?

Slate floors, stone walls, and a beamed ceiling made up the foyer which led to a living area dominated by a two-story fireplace adorned with a heavy mantle. Logs waited in the stone fireplace for a fire to be lit in the early fall mornings. Large pieces of over-stuffed brown leather furniture dominated the room. Everything complemented. Western art drew the eye up and around the room. Dianne turned in a slow circle. "I don't know what to say."

"Nothing. Don't say anything." Kip took her hand and tugged her to him, then groaned, bent his head, and kissed her without restraint. His lips and tongue sought hers with demand. His hands searched and moved beneath her jacket. He pulled her closer.

She pressed against him, trying to mold herself to him. Passion and need drove her. She returned his kiss without reservation. She traced her fingertips over every plane of his face and broke the kiss. "Kip, Kip. I…what are we doing?"

"Damned if I know." He pulled away and shook his head. "I've been wanting to do that ever since I saw you in the barn. Crazy, right?"

Not so crazy to me. "What are you saying?"

He let out a long sigh. "Nothing, really. I just wanted to kiss you. It doesn't tear down the wall between us."

A shaft of pain pierced her heart. "I know."

"I don't want to upset you, but I don't think this can work between us. What happens to me when you are finished and take off again? I won't go through that again."

Dianne couldn't argue. Hadn't she been having thoughts about leaving? *He's right.*

"Come on." Kip tugged her hand and led her to another room.

A long oak table surrounded by ten high-back chairs centered a formal living and dining space. French doors opened into the red kitchen. Clean, sleek, granite countertops reflected small appliances. She looked around, ran her hands over the smooth surface and picked up a white tea towel. Years of unspent tears clogged her throat, refusing to fall. She squeaked when she tried to talk. Her voice was soft and reverent when she did. "It's our dream kitchen. The one we sketched and colored in spiral notebooks. You've even used it in the decorations."

"I kept my notebooks. Still have 'em. When I got the ranch and was able to build, I pulled them out of the back of my closet. I never gave up on us. God knows I tried. I was angrier than I've ever been when you left. I couldn't understand or wrap my mind around why you would leave me. I still don't know. One day you were in my arms, and we were talking about our dreams. The next day you were gone. I drank and stayed drunk. Ricochet saved me from that hell. I haven't trusted another woman since then." Kip clenched his jaw and dry-washed his face with one hand.

Dianne stood before him with tears streaming down her face. "Kip."

He held up a hand signaling her not to talk. "Don't say anything. I have to finish getting this all out. I still love you, but I don't trust you. I get angry when I think of back then, but it doesn't consume me anymore. I'm afraid of being betrayed but wanting to be with you overrides the fear. My only question is why. Why did you leave?"

Dianne moved to the breakfast table. She sat down and patted the bench seat. Reaching up, she took his hand. She whispered and her voice shook with emotion. "Jocelyn is the only one who knows what I'm telling you. Please, don't interrupt me. Just let me get it out. I got the scholarship offer several weeks before I left. At the time I didn't think much of it. I stuck it in a drawer because I still planned on going to school with you. One morning, when the class was planning our graduation ceremony, I saw you in the hall. That cheerleader.... I can't remember her name...."

She ducked her head and wiped her hands on the front of her jeans.

"Misty?"

"Yeah. Misty. Anyway, she was with you. Wearing her cute little uniform. The two of you were laughing and acting goofy, pretending to dance. Your arms were around her waist. I knew I would never be able to compete with her beauty and popularity. You deserved more than a poor girl whose mother died while her father sat in a prison cell. Basically, an orphan. So, I left." The sad look of disbelief in Kip's eyes caused an ache in her heart Dianne wasn't sure she could survive.

"God, Dianne. There was never anything between me and Misty. We had been friends since kindergarten. Our moms were best friends. You've been gone for fifteen years because of Misty? I always loved you. I admired your ability to rise above the junk in your life. It makes me mad, no furious, you could even think such a thing and not talk to me about it. You are more than—have always been more than—your dad. And I loved your mom as much as you did!"

"I don't know why I thought there was something going on. I just thought—tried to convince myself actually—the two of you could make a more successful couple. You know how much I struggled with self-esteem and all back then. I really believed I would keep you from achieving your own dreams of ranching. Seeing you two together brought those thoughts home for me."

Kip's jaw tightened. "You just left. Without a damn word."

"I'm sorry. I've always regretted my decision. I was young and stupid."

He shook his head. "Being young has nothing to do with it. We have to get to the round-up. Let's go."

Just like that, he shut her out. He'd wanted to show her he'd used their plans for his home. Would he ever trust her? What's the point in staying if he didn't?

* * * *

All eyes turned their direction when they came out the back door. Kip pulled his hat low, looked to the working corral and walked toward it. Neither of them touched or said another word. Just before they reached the ranch hands, Kip took Dianne's elbow, squeezed her arm, and mouthed, "I'm sorry." His eyes begged for understanding.

She returned his smile and walked to the tent where Jocelyn waited.

Dianne went to Emperor and skidded to a stop. He was tacked out in the saddle she admired the day before. She rubbed her hand over the seat. Tears filled her eyes, and she looked for Jocelyn. "Did you do this? This saddle looks amazing on him."

Jocelyn squeezed Dianne's shoulders. "You seemed to love it so much. I bought it and arranged to have it sent out here and to get someone to put it on your horse."

"You're the best!" Dianne hugged Jocelyn, mounted Emperor, and kicked him off in a trot. He neighed, stretched his neck, and pointed his ears to the pen of calves. She rode to Kip and waited for instructions about where to go

Chapter 10

Kip whistled. Several wranglers moved to mount.

Dianne stretched forward to give Emperor a sugar cube. Turning to Kip, she smiled. "Isn't he the greatest?"

"We'll see how great he is when he's keeping calves from the gate."

Leather creaked, bridles and bits jangled, and wranglers shouted. Hooves kicked up clouds of dust. Cowboys whistled and slapped coiled ropes against their thighs as they separated the first group of agitated cows from their frightened calves. The first calf was roped, thrown to the ground with a thud, branded, tagged, vaccinated, and castrated before being sent to the chute and back to his bawling mother.

Dianne wrinkled her nose at the smell of burning flesh and hair. She pulled a red bandana over the lower half of her face. A routine was quickly established. The whistle of a lasso circling the air then falling around a calf's neck became the signal that the next calf was being worked. Emperor moved from side to side, forward, and back to keep calves away from the gate. Dianne quickly learned her role and pointed Emperor at a calf then let him do the work. She left the reins loose to give him his head.

Jocelyn stood along the fence with her mouth and nose inside the collar of her shirt and her eyes wide. Her hands clutched the top fence rail. Dianne knew she must be shocked, and probably appalled, at the sights, sounds, and smells before her. She rode to the fence. "It's all right. The calves aren't really hurt when they're bulldogged. Mostly scared because they've been separated from their mothers. Maybe you would be more comfortable helping Teresa in the chow tent. I have to get back before Kip has my head, but we'll be taking a break soon."

Jocelyn sniffed. "I hope you're right. About it not hurting them I mean."

* * * *

The cowboys took their first break. They tied their horses near a trough and loosened the cinches. Joining them, Dianne pushed her hat back letting the leather chin straps tighten to keep it from falling. She rubbed her right thigh and did several side lunges to relieve the tightness in her hips. Her thigh ached anytime she exerted herself. A constant reminder of young love and stupid accidents. She smiled, remembering the ATV wreck she and Kip had on the river bottom when they were kids.

Kip strode toward her. She welcomed him with a full-faced smile. The day filled her with pure joy. "This is great, Kip. Riding and working the calves all came back to me. Like a bicycle. Did you see the fine saddle Jocelyn surprised me with?"

Kip ran his hand up and down her arm. He kissed her on the cheek before wiping a smudge of dirt from her face with his bandana. "It's nice. You look comfortable and right on it."

"Jocelyn doesn't seem to be doing very well. I think we should check on her."

They found her in the far corner of the tent with her back to the group. She stood, her spine ramrod straight. Dianne touched her on the shoulder. "Hey, are you alright?"

Jocelyn spun, pale and shaking. Fear clouded her eyes. She shook her head and dropped her arm, her phone clutched in her hand.

Dianne wrapped her arm around Jocelyn's shoulder. "What's wrong? Is it your mother?"

Jocelyn opened her mouth to speak but no words came forth.

Knowing something was terribly wrong, Dianne took Jocelyn's hand and guided her to a bench. Kip handed Jocelyn a bottle of cold water. His eyes searched Dianne's. She shrugged and motioned him away. "J., you have to tell me what's wrong. You're scaring me. Did the branding upset you?"

Jocelyn handed Dianne her phone. A text message lit up the screen. "You need to read this."

Dianne's heart threatened to stop then settled like a rock in her chest.

I've been watching you and Dianne. Give her a message for me. Tell her I saw her and that damn cowboy this morning. I never knew she was such a slut. Have her meet me at the Brinkman Hotel in Wichita Falls. You tell her if she doesn't, she'll be sorry.

"Oh, my God." Her knees threatened to buckle. Her throat tightened. *No way in hell am I going to meet him!* Kip came toward them. She shoved the phone back into Jocelyn's hand. "Don't say anything. Not yet."

"What's up?" Kip's gaze moved from one woman to the other. "Ladies?"

"Nothing really. Jocelyn just got some bad news. It'll be fine. Could I take her to the house?" Dianne sought Kip's eyes, hoping nothing about her reflected the terror assaulting her mind. The tight-chested rise of panic threatened to take control.

Kip caressed Dianne's cheek. "Go to the house but don't go away. Don't give in to whatever's going on. I'm here." He turned, put his thumb on his forefinger and waved in a motion indicating everything would work out and walked back to the corral.

Dianne clutched Jocelyn's hand and led her to the house. She released the breath she had been holding in an audible whoosh. "My God, he's watching us. But how?"

"I don't know."

"Did he call? Do you think he's found out where I live? How could he know where we are?" She spewed questions like a .50 caliber machine gun firing from a high perch. Her knees shook, and her gut threatened to spew out everything she'd eaten in protest. Her heart beat so fast she thought it would explode. Dianne pressed a hand to her roiling stomach and took deep breaths. *Good Lord, I can't hyperventilate now. I'll faint.*

Jocelyn brought her arms up and clawed her fingers through her hair. "I checked my messages. Nothing showed up on caller I.D., that alarmed me. I opened the text right after I came back from the corral."

"Did you reply?"

Jocelyn shook her head.

Dianne wrung her hands. "Let's think about this. I don't doubt anything he said because he can be so ruthless. He's like a snapping turtle. He never lets go. Why can't he get over his pride and anger because I embarrassed him? I just wanted a divorce."

She moved to the window and looked around the work area, stopping on every face. Some she recognized. Some she didn't. Kip would never allow anyone to come to a workday that he didn't know, invite, or hire. Only friends were allowed at the dance and feast. She called Teresa. "Hey girl, will you come meet us at the house?"

"Sure. What's up?"

"Is anyone here today that you don't know?"

Teresa paused and pointed to a cowboy roping a calf in the corral. "I don't think so. There's a new wrangler who's only been here a couple of weeks. He seems nice enough. His name's Chet Sullivan. Dianne, why are you so upset? What's going on?"

Dianne rubbed at the tension building in the back of her neck. "I'll tell you when you get here, but, first, will you go back to the tent and see if there is anyone acting differently or suspicious?"

Teresa turned on her heel. "OK."

Dianne broke down in sobs that seemed to come from her soul. *How could this be happening? Why is this happening?* She reached for Jocelyn.

Jocelyn grabbed a box of tissues on the side table and passed them to Dianne. "Okay, now, get a grip. I'm pissed, and scared just like you, but we have to face this calmly."

Teresa arrived carrying a plate of fruit and cookies. "I didn't see anyone acting suspicious, but there's a kid from the catering company who seems nervous. I can find out who he is. Now, I'll get back out there and keep my eyes and ears open. Make sure you eat something. Kip probably has milk in the refrigerator to go with the cookies."

Dianne chuckled when Teresa gave her the plate and turned to go. "Thanks, you are special."

Jocelyn looked at her with widened eyes and a frown. "Why on God's green earth are you laughing?"

Holding the plate higher, Dianne answered. "Some things never change. Everyone around here thinks food will take care of anything and everything. It's the glue of the Bible Belt, especially if it's something sweet."

Dianne stood by the fireplace and Jocelyn sunk into the over-stuffed leather love seat. The food Teresa insisted they take with them sat untouched. Jocelyn's cell phone chirped announcing a second message.

I watched you on the balcony of your house, Dianne. Why are you wearing such lowly clothes? No one dismisses me or leaves me. Ever.

"I don't know what to do. If I meet him I'll be playing into his hand. If I don't, he may do something crazy. What I want to do is tell Kip. Should I?" Dianne rubbed her sweaty palms on the front of her jeans. Tears filled her eyes once more, brimmed, and fell softly to her cheeks.

"When he called the other day, he ranted about how my panic after the mugging made him look bad. He said I had shamed him because he found out from his secretary. And he was furious because I sold my condo and moved without notifying him. Why should I? We're divorced. Be careful, Jocelyn, he's using you too. I'm afraid he'll really hurt someone."

Jocelyn leaned forward and rested her elbows on her knees. "You should definitely tell Kip. This is his home. I think Simon paid someone to spy on us."

The dog barked. Footsteps and the tell-tale clink of spurs sounded on the porch.

"Kip's here." Dianne stood, rocked back on her heels, and stuffed her hands in her pockets. "What do I say?"

"You tell him the truth. Leave nothing out."

Kip entered, tossed his hat on a chair, reached down to pet the dog, and joined Dianne in front of the fireplace. He nodded at Jocelyn sitting rigid on the edge of the loveseat. Tension thickened the air.

"We received a troubling text message." Dianne whispered. She refused to make eye contact.

"What's it about? Tell me what's going on."

Dianne pulled her shoulders back, lifted her chin, and looked into his narrowed-but-concerned eyes, hoping her own did not reveal her fear. "I have to talk to you about my ex-husband, Simon."

She fell into Kip's arms when he pulled her near. He didn't say a word, just wrapped her in his embrace. He bent down, kissed her temple, and whispered in her ear. "I need to know what's going on. Something is clearly wrong. Besides, this is my house. My ranch. Come on, Dianne, don't run away again. Let me help you."

She clung to him for a split second then pulled away. *God, I don't know what to do. I want to tell him and let him take care of it. I still love him.* She looked at Kip, then to Jocelyn. Sighing, she sat down. "Kip, could I speak to Jocelyn alone just for a moment?"

"Yeah." Kip turned and went into the kitchen.

"What do you think? Should I tell him?"

Jocelyn pulled the phone out of her pocket and read the message again. "You bet you should tell him. Everything. If you turn him away now, he'll perceive it to be another betrayal. The trust you're gaining will be shattered, and you'll lose him again. Just when he's opening his heart to you."

"Do me a favor. Will you get Beth and Teresa? I think we need to be in the open about this whole thing." She blew her dearest friend a shaky kiss and joined Kip in the kitchen as Jocelyn called the other two ladies.

Within moments of returning to the living room, Kip answered a knock on the door. A young man stood on the porch with a tray of assorted pastries and a carafe of coffee. "Yeah, what do you want? We're busy here."

The kid's hands shook. The carafe and platter rattled on the tray. "Well, sir. I just thought you and the ladies would want some refreshments. Maybe, some coffee. It is cool out there. Anyway, here you go."

Kip took the tray, closed the door with his boot and moved back into the room. He set the tray on the coffee table then stepped back out onto the porch and watched the guy scurry off. He pinched his nose. Ropes of doubt and anger strangled him as he fought for an answer. *I think Dianne is in danger. She wants to talk about something. She needs to trust me now.* He looked out to the corral, walked the length of the porch several times, and noticed Teresa returning to the house with Beth. He waved at them and turned, offering a smile to Dianne who watched from a narrow opening in the window blinds. He opened the door and waited for the ladies to go inside.

Chapter 11

Dianne had watched Kip pace the length of the porch with the dog on his heels. Despite the fear she was stuffing down, she couldn't believe the sense of calm she felt in the presence of friends. Even in the midst of Simon's threats and demands, they felt like a protective circle. "I'm sure you all want to know what's going on. My ex-husband is spying on me. He knows where I live. He's threatening me. Most importantly, he's threatening all of you."

Kip took her hand. "How did he find you here?"

"I have no idea. Teresa, you probably don't know I came home because I was attacked in New York. I had some injuries, but the worst part was the panic and anxiety I couldn't shake. I ran. Sold my apartment, furniture, and most of my things, bought a car, and headed west. When I moved to Wichita Falls, I began seeing Dr. Murphy. He recommended equestrian therapy. So, here I am." Dianne pulled in a slow deep breath. "But there's more. My ex-husband sent Jocelyn a text message earlier. He's making threats. He will carry them out. He's a cruel man and must be taken seriously."

Dianne looked from person to person, stopping at Kip. He nodded to encourage her to continue.

"Beth, has anyone you didn't know come into the center lately asking about me?"

Beth put a manicured nail in her mouth and clicked it against her teeth. "No, I don't think so."

"Please be sure. He can be tricky and charming."

"A man did come in about a week ago, but he didn't ask about you. He said he wanted to talk to the owner of the center. I told him the hospital owned it and that Kip volunteered to work with the clients and horses. He didn't want to talk to him, though."

"What did he look like? Did he see any records or anything?" Dianne held her breath waiting for the answer she knew was coming.

Beth scoffed. "Well, I didn't betray any confidential information if that's what you mean."

"I'm sorry, Beth. I didn't mean to imply that at all."

"Anyway, he wasn't very tall but was dressed nicely. He had brown hair with highlights. I think it was professionally cut. His hands looked soft, even manicured. That's not something you see much of around here. He kept looking at the pictures behind my desk. There's one of you, Dianne. You and Emperor."

She couldn't form words or speak, so she nodded as red hot heat crawled up her neck and settled on her face.

Kip stood, stretched, and moved to stand behind Dianne. "Beth, was there anything on your desk or the bulletin board about today's round up?"

"Maybe. I was working on the invitation list." Beth sighed and rested her head against the sofa.

Kip curled his hands into fists. "If this SOB thinks he can harm me or anyone on my ranch he's in for a surprise." The words were hard to distinguish, given the growl with which they were delivered.

"That has to be how he found me. But how did he find out about the equestrian center? I've endangered all of you." Dianne paced the room like a caged tiger. She wasn't going down without a fight. She nodded at Jocelyn.

"I told Jocelyn I would tell you everything I know. I was a coward when I left here. I ran away, basically. The university offered me a full ride academic scholarship. That's how Joc and I met. We were roommates for six years, all through our undergraduate programs and master's degrees. We were an odd pair. Maybe that's why we became such devoted friends. Eventually, our careers landed us thousands of miles apart. I got a job in New York. She moved to San Francisco."

Dianne realized she'd made one frantic pass both ways across the floor as she whirled and started back over the same path. She took a breath and continued. "I met Simon at a fundraiser. He's an attorney at a prestigious firm—educated, debonair, and charming...when he wants to be. We married, and it didn't take long for him to show his selfish, demeaning, and controlling side. I wanted a divorce but had to wait two years for him to sign the papers. He said I was making him look bad.

"The bottom line is that he sent a text message to Jocelyn today. He described me, what I'm wearing, and even seeing me with you, Kip. He wants me to meet him, but I can't do that. I need to know what each of you thinks we should do, especially you, Kip. I think he must have a spy working for him. All of you may be in danger. He got my number and address using false pretenses. He's an angry and arrogant man. Controlling and cruel. Nobody says no to Simon Jacobson." Dianne's knees buckled and she sank down on the loveseat. Her breath hitched on a sob she tried to swallow.

"It's of utmost importance that you do not do anything to escalate this man's feelings. I know how dangerous he is." Jocelyn spoke up, making sure everyone could hear her.

Kip put his arm around Dianne. "I won't let him hurt you."

She nodded. "I know you'll try to protect me and everyone on this ranch. But how can you when we don't know where he is? He said I look good on a horse. How would he know what looking good on a horse means? He's never been near a horse. He's out there and he has someone watching all of us."

"You told us why you divorced him, but why on earth did you marry him?" Beth asked.

"That's a tougher question. I have no idea why I married him. I didn't love him. I guess I was lonely and busy at work. His law firm represents the business I worked for. I was unhappy, and his true personality frightened me. He can be brutal. I couldn't focus. I think that's why I let myself get into a position to be mugged." Her breath escaped in ragged pants.

"Wait. Are you saying you blame yourself for the mugging?" Kip questioned.

"Yes, I do blame myself. I chose to walk home from work and took a shortcut through the park. Being aware of your surroundings becomes second nature in New York. But that day, I was working on a special project and Simon was still hounding me after the divorce. The mugger came up behind me...I never saw or heard him. He grabbed my hair, put a knife to my throat, and told me to be quiet. I struggled to keep him from taking my work bag, but he ripped it from me. He cut me and beat me up. I lost consciousness and woke up in the hospital."

Kip put his hands across Dianne's shoulders and pulled her to him. "I had no idea it was that bad. Oh, God, you could have died."

Teresa hugged Kip and Dianne at the same time. A comforting six-armed-hug. She walked to the window and looked through the blinds. "I think we should try to find out if there is someone watching you. But first I need to check on my kids. The only people I don't know are a couple of the staff from the catering crew. I'll watch them."

"Beth, will you take Jocelyn and go with Teresa back out to the tent. Ask around and see if you can figure out where this ass is getting his information."

Beth nodded and the three of them left.

* * * *

Simon's hired man answered his phone on the first ring. He smiled at the promptness of this new minion. "Tell me what's going on. Things should be heating up about now."

A moment passed before the catering assistant from Wichita Falls responded. He cleared his throat. "She took her friend's phone. Looked pretty upset. They went into the house so I couldn't see anything else. Her boyfriend went in there, too."

"Do not call him her boyfriend." Simon ordered.

"Sorry, boss. I took a fresh pot of coffee and cookies to the house. I wasn't allowed past the front door."

"Did you hear anything?"

"Only voices. A man and a woman. I couldn't make out what they said."

He didn't like this arrogant country boy. "Call me immediately when she comes out of the house or find some way to get back in there."

"Yes, sir."

Simon ended the call then walked to his car to look at the photos his little spy had forwarded to him. Dianne looked happy, even comfortable. He wouldn't abide such a thing. He would never allow her to be happy.

* * * *

Once they'd watched the three ladies arrive safely at the tent, Dianne sat close to Kip with her knees angled toward him. She held his hand in a firm yet loose grip on her thigh. Tears threatened to fall again. She shook them away with an angry toss of her head. Deciding then and there to gain control of her life, she looked straight into Kip's eyes. Clearing her throat, she whispered. "I promised Jocelyn I would tell you everything. And I will. But first I must apologize for ruining your day. I realize how busy you are."

"The wranglers can handle it." Kip squeezed her hand. His eyes spoke volumes. Dianne read within them an entire range of emotion—love, fear, anger, need, and betrayal.

Kip's lips narrowed and tightened. She ran her index finger over her own lips and released a soft chuckle.

"What?"

"Your lips still do the same thing when you're mad. Just like they did when we were kids." She ran a finger over his bottom lip then ducked her head as her voice trailed off into soft, rasping words.

Kip brought her head up with two fingers beneath her chin, then pulled the other hand from her grasp before wrapping his arms around her. He pulled her to him for a sudden kiss that made her forget everything but him. Afterward, he continued to hold her, his chin resting on the top of her head.

She sighed. "He was close enough to see me riding Emperor. Either that or someone is sending him photos. Bottom line, he's out there somewhere and he's hired someone to spy for him. Simon's all about Simon. He can be brutally abusive in an emotional way. I had finally learned to be confident. He ruined that. By the time I divorced him, my self-esteem was in the gutter. I couldn't focus." Dianne dragged a hand through her hair, stood, and moved toward the kitchen.

"I need some water. Do you want anything?"

Kip followed suit and held her in place with his hands on her shoulders. "I don't need anything."

She curled against his chest and melted into its safety. His tears surprised her. Their embrace began with a comforting hug, a sweet kiss on the forehead, and a co-mingling of tears. She pulled him closer to take his mouth in a desperate kiss. A flash of wonder crossed her mind when she realized that she wanted to kiss and be kissed at a time like this.

An unwelcome knock at the door startled them. "Damn, who could that be?" Kip tried to straighten his clothes. He shoved his fingers through his hair before striding to the door.

Dianne went to the powder room. In the mirror, beard-reddened cheeks, swollen lips, and disheveled clothes greeted her. She splashed water on her face and tried to pat her hair into place. She returned to the living room to find Jocelyn holding a young man by the shoulder, and grinning ear to ear. The kid looked wide-eyed and pale. His hands shook. Dianne's gaze moved to Kip. Palpable frustration rolled from him as he eyed Jocelyn and her captive.

"You, again. What's up, Jocelyn? Who is this?"

Dianne crossed her arms over her chest, unsure if she held in anger or panic.

"This is Dennis." Jocelyn pushed the young man toward Kip. "I heard him talking real low to someone he called 'boss' and watched him for a few minutes. The shifty way he avoided eye contact with everyone and acted busy while actually snooping, made me suspicious. Since he's dressed like one of the caterers, I asked him to come pick up the trays we'd brought over earlier."

Suddenly defiant, Dennis straightened his back and looked Dianne in the eye. "Mr. Jacobson hired me to watch you and keep him informed. He got me in here pretending to be a caterer. Paid good money, too. Five grand for a couple days work. I spent it."

"Why? Did he tell you why he wanted you to watch me?" Dianne growled through teeth clenched as tightly as the fists by her side.

Dennis shrugged.

Kip stepped between the two of them and grabbed Dennis by the collar, yanking him up on his toes as they went eye to eye and toe to toe. "You little SOB, where is he?"

"I ain't sure. Nearby." Dennis jerked from Kip's grasp and straightened his collar.

"He's been looking to the west since I found him," Jocelyn offered.

"Dianne, you and Jocelyn stay in the house." Kip pointed at Dennis. "You're going to take me to him. Call and tell him you need to talk in person."

When Dennis hung up, Kip seized the kid's cell phone and slid it into his pocket. Using his own, he called Ricochet. "Tell the boys to finish up and meet me in the garage. We're taking the ATVs out and we're goin' packin'."

Kip crossed the room, unlocked an armoire, and took his handgun from a shelf. He pocketed some ammunition and smiled at Dianne. "Don't worry. We'll be back before you know it. Let me take your phone, Jocelyn. To show Sam."

Chapter 12

Tension, fear, and stress filled the kitchen where Dianne and Jocelyn waited for Kip and Ricochet.

Dianne busied herself making coffee. She searched the cabinets for supplies and found them across the room from the coffeemaker. She held up the stack of filters. "Good grief, look at this. There's no rhyme or reason in this kitchen. Just like a man." The coffeemaker groaned and sputtered to life, emitting the smell of freshly ground brew.

Jocelyn opened and closed various cabinet doors. "Doesn't look like he has any sweetener. We'll have to use sugar. Do you want extra milk?"

"Yeah, extra milk for me. I'm worried." Dianne leaned on the counter until her cheeks touched it. The cool granite soothed her, and she tried to relax. She rubbed her temples trying to erase the first signs of a headache.

"My gosh. Will they shoot Simon? I thought the guns were just for show."

Dianne cracked her knuckles. She frowned and wrinkled her forehead. "This is Texas. Guns are everywhere and are used safely. They won't shoot Simon or Dennis. Although those two don't know that. I would love to see that little scenario play out. What worries me is that Kip doesn't realize Simon could bring him down with legal maneuverings. I'll leave again before that happens. I can't be the cause of that kind of trouble for Kip or anyone else here. Going would break my heart, and I think his, but I would do it."

"No, you won't." Jocelyn squeezed Dianne's hand.

Dianne straightened her shoulders. "Yes. Yes, I would. I will do whatever needs doing to protect Kip and my friends."

* * * *

Kip and Ricochet roared along the riverbank. Dennis rode behind Kip and the two ATV's sent sand and pebbles flying in their wake. Skidding to a halt, Kip pointed to a clump of mesquite bushes and nodded at Ricochet.

Ricochet stopped his vehicle, jumped off, and ran toward the mesquites. He stopped beside a boulder and motioned for Kip. "Fresh tire tracks."

Kip pulled Dennis off the ATV by his shirt collar. He wheeled him around and stared at him with narrowed eyes that pinned Dennis in place while Ricochet continued to search the area. "Do those tire tracks belong to your reptilian boss?"

Dennis couldn't feign bravado a minute more. His shoulders slumped and he looked down. "Can't be sure. Probably."

Kip pushed him aside, making him stumble. "You're the most worthless SOB I've ever met. Bar none. Let's hear what Ricochet knows."

Ricochet rounded the bushes, hat in hand. He rubbed sweat and dirt from his face with a bandana. "Someone's been out there recently. The footprints aren't from boots or tennis shoes. Looks like men's slick-bottomed dress shoes. If it's Simon he hasn't been gone long."

Digging in the pocket of his work jacket, Kip pulled out the phone he'd taken from Dennis and threw it at him. "Call him. Right now. Find out where he is and don't even think about mentioning us." He gave the kid a stare that should have turned him to ice. "Trust me, kid, I'll know if you do."

The boy shook so hard as he keyed in the number, he had to hold the phone with both hands. The color drained from his face. He looked like a sickly Halloween ghost. For a split second Kip almost felt sorry for him. After all he was just a dumb kid. *Guess he finally figured out we mean business.*

"Hello. Mr. Jacobson? You asked me to call if I learned anything more. I think it would be best if we meet somewhere to talk. It's private. And, important."

Dennis listened. "Yes, sir. Of course."

"He's at the fish house. Said watching those people at the ranch made him hungry." He handed the phone back to Kip, bent over at the waist, and vomited.

Anger and acid boiled in Kip's blood. He hauled in two deep, controlling breaths, hoping to calm himself. He had to be in control when he faced the damn bastard. He nodded at Ricochet. "Call Sam and tell him to meet us at the fish house."

Ricochet grinned at Dennis.

"Who's Sam?" Dennis asked.

Kip turned the key and the ATV roared to life. "Shut up and get on. You'll find out soon enough."

They drove through the sand, up the riverbank, and crossed the highway into the parking lot of the restaurant.

Kip took off his hat and used it to brush dust off his shirt and chaps before entering the café. "Dennis, you're going in first. Sit across from that SOB. We'll be right behind you."

Ruth greeted Kip and Ricochet and raised an eyebrow at the frightened kid with them.

Dennis walked to a booth and sat across from a well-dressed man who matched Beth's description.

Simon put his fork down and took a large drink of ice water. "You know, this isn't bad for hick food. I'm pretty sure the water isn't filtered and there's some strange sounding things on the menu. Calf fries? What are they?"

Dennis stifled a laugh and told him about calf fries.

Simon wrinkled his nose. "Now, why were you so desperate to speak to me? That was certainly not a part of my plan."

Kip and Ricochet approached the booth with creaks of leather chaps and the song of spurs. Simon looked up at them. "Excuse me, can I help you?"

Kip slid in next to Dennis and Ricochet sat next to Simon.

"What's the meaning of this? I did not invite you to sit here. You both smell bad." Simon wrinkled his nose and sniffed in disgust.

"I'm sure we don't smell too good to a Pretty Boy like you. We've been working cattle. It's sweaty work jumping off of a horse when it skids to a stop, throwing a calf to the ground, branding it, and cutting its nuts off. Most of the time we get shit on, and we always get slobbered on. What you smell is real work."

Simon's lips thinned to a line like kids drew on stick figures. "Care to introduce me to your friends, Dennis? If you expect more money out of me, you are dead wrong. I'll sue you for extortion." He drew each word out, articulating it to dictionary perfection with an air of superiority.

Kip looked at the young man, who was clearly scared to the marrow of his bones. He had paled to a shade of green that usually preceded vomiting. He shook so hard his teeth rattled.

"Well, Sir . . . I ain't wanting no more money. This is Kip Mahan. The man next to you is called Ricochet. They found out about you and forced me to bring them here." Dennis stammered and stumbled over his words. He reached for the water and gulped until the glass was half empty.

The waitress moved to the booth. "You boys ready to order?"

"Not yet. We'll let you know." Kip flashed a mischievous grin and winked at Ruth.

Simon straightened his tie and reached for another piece of fish. "What do you gentlemen want? Dennis and I have been communicating but there's no crime in that. I know who you are, Mr. Mahan. I don't give a damn who you are, Mr. Ricochet."

"Yeah, we know who you are too, Mr. Jacobson." Kip looked up when the bell above the door clanged. Sam came to the booth. Kip stood to shake his hand.

"How you doin'? What's up?" Sam pulled his jacket aside, revealing his badge and weapon.

Simon lifted his chin and sniffed. His face was flushed. "Officer, these men have threatened me. I want them arrested."

"It's Sheriff. Sheriff Sam Walker. What have they done to you? Seems Kip wants you arrested for stalking and trespassing."

Simon's hands slapped the table causing the red plastic basket of fish and fries to fall in his lap. He tried to stand, shrieked, and attempted to rub the greasy stain off the front of his silk shirt with a napkin. "This is the most absurd thing I've ever heard. I am W. Simon Jacobson, Esquire. Who am I supposed to be stalking and when did I trespass? I am a managing partner at Jackson, Jacobson, and Endicott Law Firm in New York City. Tread lightly, gentlemen."

Sam turned to Kip and spit brown tobacco into a cup. "Your turn."

"This is Dianne's ex-husband. He called and threatened her. He's stalking her. He came here from New York because he can't stand folks who won't bend to his will. He claims to have hired this scared jack rabbit of a kid to spy on Dianne at the round-up. He texted Dianne's friend with more threats. And he did trespass, down by the river. While you're at it, you can also arrest this boy for trespassing. He was on my ranch under false pretenses."

Sam spit into his cup again and wiped his mouth with the back of his hand. "Is this true, sir? I've never known Kip to lie."

Simon stared at Sam. "Must you spit in public, sir?"

"Well, I ain't gonna swallow it."

Everyone except Jacobson laughed.

"Sir. It is certainly not illegal to telephone or text people. I assure you I did not trespass. I was near the bridge. I did hire this young man. I merely wished for an opportunity to speak to my wife. However, she has chosen not to communicate with me. I am leaving now. Please move, Mr. Ricochet." Simon motioned to Ruth to bring the tab.

Ricochet continued to sit there, grinning at the whole thing. He shifted, making sure his spur scraped Simon's leg. "Sorry."

Kip handed Dennis' phone to the sheriff. "Proof is right here. He was trespassing on 3G land down in the river bottom. It's posted. I reckon if you wanted you could compare the tire tracks with those on this city slicker's rental car and his shoes. You know the place?"

Sam nodded. "That's not enough for me to arrest him. I can file trespassing charges and watch him."

"Hell, I showed you the message and told you what Dianne said. You mean to tell me you can't do anything about it?" Kip glared and swallowed the thick bile clogging up his throat at the helplessness threatening to consume him. *I'd like to beat the hell out of the bastard.* He vowed not to remain out of the loop as far as Dianne was concerned. He'd get back to the ranch, make sure she was safe, and dare anyone to harm her again. He clenched and unclenched his fists by his side. He wanted to pummel the SOB into hell.

Sam shook his head. "Like I said, I can't arrest him now. Just not enough."

"Does he have to hurt Dianne before something can be done?" Kip slammed his fist on the table.

"We'll watch him. I promise. I'll alert the Wichita Falls department."

Kip put his hat on and rose to leave the booth. He and Ricochet raised the noise level in the café with a flurry of chaps, boots, and spurs. "I'll come down and fill out those trespassing papers now."

Simon stood and stepped away from the booth. "If you gentlemen—and I use that term loosely—will excuse me, I need to get back to my hotel." The left side of his face lifted in a sneer. He brought his hand up in an awkward salute and tossed fifty dollars on the table. "Dennis, may I offer you a ride?"

Dennis paled even more and shook his head. "I'll catch a ride with the catering company."

"C'mon. I'll take you back to the ranch," Ricochet said. Dennis followed him like a scared puppy.

Kip left with Sam and watched Simon exit the building, get into a fancy car, and screech out of the parking lot.

Chapter 13

Dianne ran outside as soon as the ATVs rumbled into the yard. She stood near the porch railing and waited for Kip. "Did you find him?"

"Yeah. We did." Kip stepped into her outstretched arms.

"What happened? I've been so worried."

"I need to wash up. I'll be right out and tell you everything."

Dianne followed him in and sat next to Jocelyn on the couch while he disappeared down the hall. "My stomach is in knots. I'm jumpy. Better than anyone else, I know how brutal Simon can be. I keep wondering if I should just leave."

Jocelyn stood, reached out, and put her hands on Dianne's shoulders. "I'm going outside and let you two talk. Do. Not. Blow. This. Do you hear me? I know you're scared, I am too, but you have a rare chance to live the life you want to live."

"You are right, as usual." Dianne waited for Kip. *I wonder if I can ever truly get rid of Simon. Can Kip forgive me?*

Kip came back in, drying his hand with a towel. "Where's Jocelyn?"

"Outside."

Kip grinned and sat beside her. "You would have loved it. Simon wasn't at the place the kid expected him to be, but we tracked him down at the fish house. Dennis slipped in across from the son-of-a-bitch. Didn't take him a minute to start asking about you. I slid in next to the kid and Ricochet sat right next to Simon, blocking him in. The SOB introduced himself as an Esquire. What in God's name is an esquire anyway? I thought Satan was going to blow out of his ears. That man is full of hate. He even said we smelled."

Dianne chuckled. "I'm sure he did think you were smelly."

"I accused him of stalking and trespassing. He was pretty arrogant 'til Sam got there."

"Are you talking about Sam Walker?"

"Yeah, he's the sheriff now. But I do have something else to tell you." He rubbed his face with both hands and shook his head. "Sam had to let the bastard go. Said there wasn't enough evidence to hold him. I filed trespassing charges, but nothing will happen unless Simon is caught trespassing again. Sam's going to alert the Wichita Falls police."

Dianne put her face in her hands. Hot tears seeped between her fingers. "You've made an enemy you may regret. Simon is mean, Kip. I can't bear the thought of anything happening to you or anyone around here. I just can't handle it. Please be careful."

"We can't do anything right now. It pisses me off, but those're the facts. I'll be fine. Let's change the subject. Before long, the boys will be setting up for the dance. Will you be there?"

Dianne nodded. She didn't trust herself to speak. She hid the ups and downs complete with the twists and turns of a wild rollercoaster ride of emotions behind a smile. *That's close enough to asking me for a date, right?* The fullness of hope soared through her, darkened by sadness over the possibility of leaving again.

Kip stood and bowed with a chivalrous flare. "Well, my Lady, I'm off to the bunkhouse to clean up. I'll be back in an hour to walk you and Jocelyn to the dance."

He handed her Jocelyn's phone. "Tell her I put my number in there in case she needs anything, and I programmed hers into mine."

"OK." Dianne watched him walk out the back door. She found her purse and shook it, then reached in, fumbled around for the brown medication bottle, and dropped a pill into her hand.

You don't need this. It's becoming a crutch. Jocelyn's words about the medication echoed in her mind. Could her friend be right? Was she depending on the pills? No. No, she wasn't. Even at her wit's end, she was thinking clearly about the pills and other things. Still, she put the pill back into the bottle.

A shower revived her. The few tears she shed swirled down the drain along with shampoo suds and the filthy feelings from Simon's threats. Sitting at a vanity, she bent over to dry her hair and surprised herself by humming.

She'd just finished dressing when Jocelyn came through the door, twirled, and giggled. "Ta-Da."

"Goodness, you look great. I teased you about the fringed vest, but it works. The entire outfit makes a big statement. 'I'm not a cowgirl but I can act like one.'"

Dianne snorted with laughter. She crooked her arm into Jocelyn's elbow and led her to a floor-length mirror.

"I may not be a real Texas girl, but damn, we do look hot. I heard Kip come in a few minutes ago. I just have one thing to say. Have a good time. Let the bad crap of today slide behind you."

"I intend to have nothing but a good time."

Arm-in-arm they headed down the stairs. Dianne stopped and lost her breath when she spotted Kip waiting at the bottom. His brown suede vest hugged a crisp white shirt, tucked into starched and ironed Wranglers boasting creases sharp enough to draw blood, and shiny black boots. Kip was a cowboy just as surely as the Marlboro Man from old school television and magazine ads she studied in college.

A turquoise stone embedded in the silver belt buckle stood out in stark contrast against the black leather. *Good Lord, he should be arrested for looking so sexy.*

* * * *

Kip's mouth went dry. Had he ever seen such a stunning sight? Dianne wore a cherry-red sundress with a vee neck that exposed just enough cleavage and the hint of a scar near her throat. A reminder of the mugging. She wore black boots made for two-stepping and a gold faceted bracelet that sparkled around her thin wrist. Her hair hung loose. *Sweet Baby Jesus. I'm in trouble.* Maintaining a safe distance was going to be impossible. He cleared his throat and held out an arm for each woman. His eyes were locked on Dianne. "Ladies, shall we go?" Then, although he hadn't a clue whether Jocelyn even wore a stitch, he added, "You both look beautiful."

Couples formed around the planked, sawdust-strewn dance floor while the band tuned up. Dianne looked from face to face, smiling at each one. She closed her eyes and in an instant, saw those same faces reflecting their youthful days in high school.

Teresa with her hands behind her back and her head down. Waist-length hair draped forward and over her shoulder to hide her from other people. She was shy back then, but if someone asked her to dance, she was full steam ahead.

Josh was rarely with the same girl twice, but he could make every girl feel like she was the only one in the world. He thought he was such a stud.

And Ricochet. Some things never changed. Cocky and confident.

She hadn't felt this blessed in a long time.

A lively two-step opened the floor for dancing. Kip led Dianne away. She threw her head back and laughed. "Wow. I can still dance."

"Of course, you can still dance. You have a real man leading you." Kip twirled her around in a dizzying spin. Years and hurt fell away beneath the magic of twinkling lights in the trees. A slow waltz followed the two step. He pulled her so close a piece of paper couldn't pass between them. No words were spoken. When the song ended, he took her hand and settled on a bench near the dance floor.

She pulled the necklace she wore most of the time from the bodice of her dress and slid the pendant along the delicate chain.

"Is that the necklace I gave you?"

"It is. I've always kept it near. For a long time, I refused to take it off. I finally wrapped it in velvet and put it in my jewelry box. This seemed the perfect time to wear again."

Kip kissed Dianne on the cheek. "We had some good times. Made good memories."

"Yes, we did. And tonight, is perfect. Like a dream. I wish Simon wasn't up to no good."

"Forget about him." He touched the pendant with one finger then settled his hand over her heart. "I wish things could be the way we want them but . . ."

"But you still don't trust me." A snake wrapped around her heart and coiled in her chest.

"I want to. I want a lot of things." Kip put his fingers to her lips. He took her face in his hands and kissed her. The kiss began gently and built into a deep, soul-searching, tongues dancing, bruising tangle of mouths.

Dianne sighed. Her heart fluttered with hope.

Kip jerked away. "God, I'm sorry. I shouldn't have done that."

"No. You definitely shouldn't have, especially if you don't trust me." She stood and strode across the room to where Jocelyn was talking to a cowboy and laughing in what Dianne recognized as her "moving in for the kill" flirting.

"Jocelyn, I'm leaving. You can stay if you want to, but I am going."

Jocelyn turned a concerned gaze to her. "What is it?"

"I'm just tired."

"I'll come with you." Jocelyn favored the cowboy with a saucy wink that put a smile on his scowling face.

They gathered their things and left without saying goodbye to Kip.

Dianne opened the back door and walked with long, angry strides to her car. She dug around for the keys and spilled everything in her purse on the seat. "Damn it! Will this never end?"

Chapter 14

At home, she dragged herself up the stairs using the banister for leverage. She was bone tired. Not just physically, but her feelings and her heart hurt. She got a bottle of water from the mini fridge, twisted off the cap, threw it on the floor, and gulped down half the contents. Exhausted, she fell onto the cushions of the love seat.

"So, you want to talk about it?" Jocelyn sat beside her.

Dianne shook her head. "I just realized Kip will never trust me. I'd rather talk about something else. What did you think of working on the ranch?"

"All right, we'll talk about frivolous stuff instead of the elephant in the room. At first, I was completely out of my element. Especially near the animals. They're so big. I hated the part where the baby cows were taken from their mothers and branded. But those cowboys. Man, they're all so polite. Must be part of the cowboy code you told me about. And, those pants, the ones you call chaps that only cover the front and show off their tight, cowboy butts, like nothing I could ever imagine if I hadn't seen it with my own eyes."

Jocelyn laughed. Dianne managed a weak smile.

"Your friends are so nice. Especially Teresa. She told me she missed you the most every time she had a major milestone in her life. Her wedding. You were supposed to be her Maid of Honor. And the births of her children. Said your absence broke her heart. I felt sorry for her because I can't even imagine not having you in my life. Besides, none of them knew where you were or even if you were alive. Then… then Simon and his drama. He's the one I wish was dead."

Dianne sighed. "Guess I never thought about how my leaving would impact anyone. At least, I didn't allow myself to think about it. Much, anyway."

"Are you freaking serious? Kip is nuts about you. He's still in love with you. Probably always will be. Why can't the two of you just get over the past and start fresh?"

"I don't know. I imagine we're both scared. I want to try, but Kip doesn't. At least, it feels that way. I am thinking about leaving." Dianne put her chin in her cupped hands and rested her elbows on her knees. She looked toward her desk and got up to check it out. The computer was on, and something was propped against the screen. A note with her name printed on the front.

Her heart stopped for three beats. *Simon has been here.* Her throat closed up around a ball of thick tar. Sweat broke out from her head to her toes, even as a shiver shook her body. The few steps to her desk felt like a journey of a thousand miles. "I didn't think I left my computer on."

"What's wrong? You look like you've seen a ghost." Jocelyn rushed to Dianne's side.

"My God. Look at this. He was in here. In my home." Dianne dropped onto the desk chair and pointed to the note.

"You will not make a fool of me ever again."

Jocelyn planted her hands on her hips. "That damn son-of-a-bitch."

"When was he here? How did he get in?" Dianne's voice croaked out in a harsh whisper.

"You need to call Kip. Now," Jocelyn insisted.

"No. We should call the sheriff."

Jocelyn picked up Dianne's phone, giving her a defiant glare. "The sheriff hasn't done anything yet. He has to wait until there's evidence a law has been broken. Besides, he doesn't have jurisdiction in Wichita Falls. Does he?"

Dianne had to admit Jocelyn had a point. "You're right."

Jocelyn spoke to Kip and told him Simon had been in the apartment. "He's on the way. He's calling Sam," she said, disconnecting the call and handing the phone back to Dianne.

"I'll wait for them downstairs. Lock the door behind me." Dianne walked down to the foyer and looked out the paned glass window of the front door. She checked the latch, grateful it was locked. *How did he get in here?*

Kip arrived with Ricochet and Sam.

"Come on up. We have coffee." She handed Sam the note. "I found this propped up beside the screen of my computer. I thought I had turned it off, but it was on."

Jocelyn had coffee waiting on a tray. She pointed to the chairs. "Have a seat."

Sam put the note in a Zip-Lock bag. "How did he get in? Did he take anything?"

"I don't know how he got in. My landlady is out of town. Guess the alarm's not working again. Nothing seems to be missing. We need to think about what to do. I don't know what to say, but I know he can be clever, and he will stop at nothing to get what he wants. He doesn't make mistakes. He had a reason for telling us the name of his hotel. He has a reason for everything. Nothing goes uncalculated." She shuddered. Just the thought that he could invade her life was as scary as hell. None of this mess made a lick of sense.

"It's clear he was in your place. I'll keep this note as evidence and will come back tomorrow. Kip, take me to Mr. Jacobson's hotel. Time for me to have a chat with him." Sam put the bagged note in his pocket.

"Should I go?" Dianne stood next to Kip, grateful for his arm holding her upright.

"Nah. I've alerted the authorities here about Simon. We'll figure it out. You call that alarm company and get them out here right now." Sam tipped his white ten-gallon hat to Dianne and Jocelyn. "Oh, one other thing. Here's my card." He handed one to Diann and another to Jocelyn. "Memorize that number and call me anytime. Day or night. For anything. Understand?"

Both nodded.

Kip kissed Dianne on the cheek. "Don't worry. I'll call."

Jocelyn moved to Dianne and took her arm. "Let's go to the main kitchen and eat our weight in ice cream while we wait for the alarm company. I saw Rocky Road and Chocolate Swirl yesterday when we ate downstairs. Maybe it will help take our minds off everything."

Before they reached the bottom of the stairs, a knock sounded on the door. A service tech identified himself. Keeping the chain intact, Dianne opened the door a sliver and checked the guy's ID, then let him in. She and Jocelyn went into the breakfast room. Dianne sat in her favorite place and ran her hand over the glass-top table while Jocelyn scooped ice cream into bowls. "I love sitting in this room anytime, but late at night is the best. The way the shadows dance from the leaded glass windows and the plants transport me back in time to the 1920s when the Weeks family built the mansion. Miss Wood, the owner, loves art and the paintings throughout the house are impressive. But I love the little ones peeking out from the windowsills."

She took a big spoonful of the Chocolate Swirl ice cream Jocelyn placed in front of her, and let it melt in her mouth. After removing her boots, she rubbed her feet over the smooth, cool tile. Her pleasure dimmed when she thought about Simon—out there somewhere, too close. "I hope they find Simon before he hurts someone."

"Do you really believe Simon would do something to harm you, Kip, or me?"

"Come on, Jocelyn. You know him. You know he's harmed me. Yes. He would hurt me or anyone else who got in his way. He always gets what he wants. Now, he's focused on getting even with me. He's crossing lines I never imagined even he would cross."

"What Simon does or doesn't do isn't in your control, Dianne. Kip won't let him near you."

Dianne didn't feel as confident. She pulled a small bottle of pills from her pocket. "Kip may not be able to stop him."

She stopped eating and talking when the service technician stepped through the door and assured them the alarm was back online. Signing the paperwork he handed her, Dianne thanked him and escorted him out the side entrance. Returning to the kitchen, she picked up her bottle of pills and addressed Jocelyn once more. "Are you ready to go back upstairs? I'm fading fast. Must be the ice cream. Do you need the bathroom first? I want to wash my face and put on pajamas."

"Wait. How many of those pills have you had today? Seems like a lot."

Dianne scoffed and stood to leave. "I haven't taken more than what is prescribed. It has been a stressful day. Wouldn't you say?"

Jocelyn's reply was a noncommittal grunt.

They double-checked every door and window of the mansion to make sure all were locked, then set the alarm. Even so, the spine-tingling feeling of being watched— the one she'd experienced in the park not long ago—remained. She recalled other times she'd felt uncomfortable without a reason. Goosebumps rose on her arms. She tried to brush them away like swiping insects off with her hands. The shiver-bumps persisted and left her feeling cold. She shuddered.

Back in her suite, Dianne turned the brown bottle over and over in her hand while the water heated up for a shower. Anxiety began its ruthless attack, like a stranger with his hands around her throat. Eyes stared at her from every corner. *Maybe I have been taking too many pills.*

She looked in the mirror, afraid she would see the image of her father gazing back at her. Tonight, after the day she'd had, seemed the perfect time to take a pill. *Maybe not reason enough.*

She put the bottle in the linen closet and hid it under a stack of towels. She'd gain strength in other ways. For now, one day at a time, until Simon was taken care of. Jocelyn would stay and help her through this drama.

Chapter 15

Kip and Sam went to Simon's hotel room. Sam banged on the door until the man answered. When the door opened, Sam clenched his teeth, gripped Simon by the collar, and pushed him into the room. "You dirty, arrogant Scum Bag. I've just come from investigating a break-in at Dianne's place. Know anything about that?"

"I could have you arrested for assault. I don't know anything. The bitch probably planted it to frame me. Besides, aren't you the Sheriff in that hick town?"

"I am. But the Wichita Falls police department knows I'm here and they'll be joining us. I'll give you two choices. You either leave town for good, or you will be investigated for breaking and entering. Could be a very long time before you go back to your cushy city life."

"Oh, I think I'll take my chances. No smalltown yokel is going to threaten me and get away with it."

Sam released him and shrugged. He tipped his hat. "Suit yourself. You can expect a visit from some detectives soon. Nothing small town about them."

Simon pasted a satisfied grin on his face. Kip wanted to wipe the smirk off with his fists. He kept his hands in his pockets, clenched and ready to strike like a coiled rattlesnake.

* * * *

Dianne paced, waiting for Kip's call. She seesawed between shaking and crying. Simon would likely call in his high-profile friends. Dread came to a slow boil in her chest, making breathing difficult. She caught a look of concern from Jocelyn and smiled. "It will be all right. I've got this."

"I know. I can't help but worry. I know Simon."

The phone vibrated in Dianne's hand. She answered right away. "Kip?"

She listened to him, maintaining eye contact with Jocelyn until the conversation ended. "It seems Simon tried to intimidate Sam. Not a good move. Detectives from Wichita Falls will pay him a visit tomorrow. The fight may really begin if…no, *when* Simon's friends fly down here. I'm sure he's going to call in the muscle now and they're as ruthless and venomous as he is."

Jocelyn waved a deprecating hand. "I have a feeling Simon may be surprised at the intelligence and courage of the men around here. He may even work out some kind of plea deal just to get back on that private jet to New York."

Dianne nodded, hoping Jocelyn was right while trying to squelch the fear that she wasn't. "Let's try to get some sleep."

Chapter 16

The next morning Simon found himself sitting across a scarred and wobbly wooden table from two detectives. He looked them in the eyes. "It's clear you don't have enough evidence to hold me. I refuse to answer any of your inane questions until my attorneys arrive from New York."

The detectives looked at each other and grinned. "Did he just call our questions insane…or inane? Pot and kettle black, don't you think? Fine with us. Stay away from Dianne Raborn Jacobson and don't leave town."

Simon roared with laughter. "Yesterday that stupid sheriff told me to leave town. Now, you're telling me to stay. Which is it?"

"Well, now that you're officially a suspect, you'd be wise to stay around."

Simon stood, buttoned his suitcoat, and scooted the chair under the table. "Gentlemen. Until later, then."

He slammed the door on the way out.

* * * *

Simon told the hotel staff a friend of his would be checking in, but he was checking out for the time being. He smiled and swaggered to his car and drove to the apartment across from the mansion. The cops wouldn't be able to track him. His muscle man would see to that.

He poured a double shot of top-shelf Scotch whisky. He would abide by the agreement to stay away from Dianne. For now. However, he would do some damage to the cowboy. Arrangements had been made for his friend to fly west.

Someone knocked on the door. Ahh...his guest already. Simon opened the door and greeted Larry. He expected the man to be standing there in an ill-fitting suit with a cigar hanging out of the corner of his mouth. Instead, he saw a clean-shaven man dressed like a cowboy. Right down to the hat and boots. But the never fully smoked cigar was there. He laughed and waved him in. "You may be taking this too far."

Larry sat at the table. He extinguished his cigar against the side of a fragile bone china cup before stowing it in his pocket. "Nah. It's important to blend in. I read about cowboys on the plane. So, what's this job that has me flying across the country and paying me thousands more than my usual fee?"

"I came out here to get Dianne. She had the nerve to leave New York without contacting me. I figured she would come back here since it's her hometown. She's returned to her first love. They're a little too chummy. I want something to happen to the cowboy. Not fatal. Just give him a message to stay away from my wife."

"Let me get this straight. You want me to mess with the cowboy but leave Dianne, your ex-wife, alone."

Simon nodded and handed the man a folded paper torn form a yellow legal pad. "Yes. For now. Just follow Dianne and try to figure out her habits. My plan for her will be phase two. Here's the information. Names and addresses. I have a hotel room for you down the road. The key is taped inside the note. Don't contact me until you have a plan."

* * * *

Larry called in less than two hours. "I have a plan. I'll meet you in a few minutes."

Simon disconnected and waited. This episode would end soon, but not before he made his mark. He knew Larry would have a perfect plan. A memorable plan. He chuckled when he heard the knock.

"Come on in. I poured you a whisky. What's the grand plan?" Simon took a folder and pointed the other man to a chair.

Larry sipped his whisky and grinned. "I looked at the maps you sent. I think I can get to one of Mahan's pastures without trespassing along the river. Thought I might shoot some of his cows. I learned on the plane that cowboys are pretty serious about their livestock. It might damage his pocketbook. I used my binoculars and saw that I would have easy access to the foreman if the first plan don't work. Ricochet, you said? Do you want Mahan hurt? It'll be easy to watch Dianne. I managed to look over the fence at the mansion. Man, that place is huge! Anyway, there's a gate and back door to the basement. There are security signs all over the joint, so I'll have to be careful."

"Start with the cattle. Call me as soon as you have news. I don't have to remind you of our agreement, do I?"

"Nah, consider it done."

Chapter 17

Dianne sat in the dark and leaned into the plump cushions of the loveseat. Knowing Jocelyn had agreed to stay longer helped calm her. Having her near offered a comfort she couldn't put into words. She gathered her hair into a messy bun and held it in place with a pencil.

"What are you thinking?" Jocelyn yawned and rubbed her eyes.

"I can't help but worry about Kip. It's not too much of a stretch to think Simon will go after him in whatever way he can." She stood and walked to the window, pulled the curtain back to gaze at the full Hunter's moon, stunning in the clear sky and surrounded by stars. You couldn't see moons like this in the city. She would miss this when, *if,* she left.

* * * *

Kip stood on his porch and stared at the moon wishing Dianne was with him. His body and heart ached for her. He couldn't decide if he was happy or scared to death. Probably both. He wanted to trust her, but something told him she would be gone in a New York minute the first time a blip popped up in their new relationship. He bent down to pet his dog who stared at him with full devotion and acceptance. "Come on, boy. Let's go inside."

Though late, he needed to hear Dianne's voice. His blood ran cold every time he thought of that son-of-a-bitch, Simon. He smiled when she answered the phone, her voice soft and husky. "You awake?"

"Yeah. Couldn't get to sleep. My mind is racing like a hamster on a wheel. Are you okay?"

"Yeah, just getting ready to hit the sack." Kip stifled a yawn.

"Jocelyn's still here. We finished off two containers of ice cream in the last couple of nights. Have you heard any more about Simon?"

"The detectives spoke with Simon. They're watching him. My intuition and gut is working overtime. I don't trust him. I've told the hands to carry guns and be on the lookout for strangers or anything that doesn't feel right." He blew out a breath.

"That's good. Don't let your guard down until this mess is over. Are you still coming to town tomorrow? I'm going to the center to spend time with Emperor."

"I'll be there. Go to bed now. Get some rest."

"Thanks for calling. I wanted—no, I needed to hear your voice."

Kip hung up the phone thinking about how soft and dreamy Dianne sounded.

* * * *

Dianne arrived at the center an hour early. Despite the threat of Simon hanging over her head, she felt good. Emperor and Kip waited for her. A sudden surge of happiness made her laugh out loud. "Good morning, guys. I have something for you." She gave Emperor a sugar cube and kissed Kip on the cheek.

Kip draped his arm over her shoulder. "You sure are chipper this morning, especially for someone who had such a rough few days. Where's Jocelyn?"

She shrugged. "She decided to stay home and chill. I refuse to let Simon ruin my day. I'm leaving it all to Sam and the detectives. I hope they can gather enough evidence to arrest him."

Kip nodded. "Let's hope. In the spirit of putting all the b.s. aside for the day let's take a ride. I'll saddle the horses. I want to show you the back pasture. There's a nice oak tree waiting for someone to come along with a picnic basket. Which, by the way, I happen to have packed. You game?"

"A ride *and* a picnic? Hell, yeah." Dianne opened the door to Emperor's stall and brushed him before Kip came back to saddle him. She looked down the stable aisle and watched the man who never left her heart leading a big palomino out of the last stall. Holding Emperor's lead, she closed her eyes and breathed deeply.

The smell of hay, manure, leather, and her perfume filled the air. For the first time in years, she felt the stirring of a new life building in her heart. Coming home felt right despite Simon and the aftermath of the mugging.

Kip saddled both horses. "Ready? Calm down, Butternut." He mounted and tugged on the reins of his horse when she side-stepped and pawed the ground.

Dianne laughed. "Looks like your horse is ready."

"Seems to be, doesn't she?"

The high grass waved to and fro with every breeze. The horses snatched bites as they walked through the pasture. Emperor tossed his head when another horse whinnied. Dianne stretched forward and rubbed his neck. "This is nice. I kept myself busy through school and life in New York so I wouldn't have a chance to miss this."

"Today is all about relaxing, sharing memories, and the fried chicken I have in this basket. There's our picnic tree." Kip pointed to a towering oak that provided a haven of shelter from the sun and an opportunity to just breathe without worry.

They dismounted, loosened the cinches, removed the bridles, then haltered the horses and tethered them. He pulled a blanket from his saddlebag and handed it to her. "Take this over to the tree. I'll get the rest."

Dianne shook the folds from the blanket and straightened it. She put rocks on each corner and sat down cross-legged. Closing her eyes, she breathed in the smell of home.

"Here we go. Let's see what else we have in here. No telling because Teresa packed it." He held up a chicken leg, an apple, cookies, Hershey's kisses. and a container of macaroni salad.

"Teresa remembered that I love macaroni salad." Moments passed in peaceful silence while they ate.

Dianne rubbed her stomach and lay back on the blanket. "Look at the clouds."

"What do you see? You used to have a wild imagination."

She pointed upward and turned to smile at Kip. "That group looks like a stampeding herd of horses. Or it could be a weird Rorshach blot."

"A what? A blot? What the hell is that? I agree about the horses."

She laughed. "Rorshsach blots are blobs of ink that shrinks use to help diagnose issues. The doctor in New York had me look at some. I swear they all just looked like someone spilled a bottle of ink. I flunked that test."

Kip turned on his side, took Dianne in his arms, and kissed her forehead. "Enough of the clouds." He began brushing kisses down her face, first on one side, then the other. Finally, after a brush of his lips across her nose, he pulled her close and kissed her deeply.

She tried to snuggle against his chest when he ended the kiss.

He pulled away and stood up so fast the picnic basket tipped over. "Sorry, I got carried away. No regrets, but we should be getting back."

In an instant, the magic was gone. Again. He'd built the wall around himself.

"Did I do something wrong? It seems you're confused or conflicted or something. Be honest with me. Tell me what you want. What is keeping you back? I have decided to stay here, even if you choose not to have anything to do with me. I am home with or without you. I will say this though, I do still love you. I do still want us to begin again. But not if you can't decide what you want or don't want."

Dianne blinked back tears. She stood in front of him with her hands on her hips. *Damned if I'm going to cry in front of him.*

"Oh, hell. I am afraid. But not of you or even us. I am scared half to death about Simon and what he might do. I want to protect you and if that means losing you again, I'll do it."

"I understand, but stop shutting me out because of Simon. I won't push you, but I expect you to stop acting like a wishy-washy teenager. Now, let's get back to the barn." Dianne blinked away tears and helped Kit gather supplies and tack up the horses. They rode back in tense silence. Even so, it felt like a bridge had been crossed.

"I'm not trying to shut you out. I'm struggling. So much has happened. I want Mr. Esquire and his bullies behind bars. Maybe on Jupiter or something. Mostly, I want you. I want the life we dreamed about. The years have passed for both of us. How about we go steady again? Start over." Kip pulled Dianne to him for a quick kiss. The horses cooperated and moved closer together.

Dianne pulled the necklace out of her shirt collar. "Remember you gave me this when you asked me to go steady in the tenth grade? You were nervous. I was scared I was going to lose my lunch. But I said, 'yes.' What do I say now about going steady?"

She smiled and hesitated a moment just to tease him. "I say yes. Again."

Chapter 18

Kip caught a flash of light from the hill across from the pasture holding his heifers. He looked again and didn't see anything. He slapped a coiled lasso against his thigh to coerce several steers into a holding pen. Then he dismounted and locked the gate.

Ricochet drove like a banshee was after him. Dust flew from the truck and trailer when he braked to a screeching halt. He jumped out of the vehicle before the engine completely stopped. "Kip! Come with me—now. Someone's shot ten of our prize heifers in the pasture. The others are bawling and wanting to stampede. The boys are trying to calm them down. They're moving them through the chute to get them to the corral by the barn. Some of them wanted to pull the dead ones out with the tractor but I told them to wait. Goddam it. The bastard used some kind of long-range rifle."

Kip loaded his horse in the trailer and climbed in the cab. He fisted his hands and hit the dashboard. "When? Not long ago I saw flashes of light from the hill on the west. Didn't think much about it."

"I don't know who did this, but I guarantee we'll catch the SOB. He'll be sorry. Someone called Sam. He'll be out here as soon as he can."

"Dianne. My God, Dianne. I have to call her." Kip's stomach rolled and acid rose in his throat. He used speed dial, but Dianne's phone went straight to voice mail. He left a message and tried Jocelyn. It went straight to voice mail. "They aren't answering."

"I imagine they're fine."

"You know as well as I do Simon is behind this. No one around here would shoot up a pasture of heifers."

"Keep trying to get hold of Dianne. All we can do is wait on Sam."

Kip flew out of the truck while Ricochet parked it. He ran to the huddle of cowboys standing beside the gate of the pasture full of blood and death. They held rifles and watched the hills. Each of them tipped his hat to Kip.

"Boys, any idea what we have going on here?"

"No. We came to check on them and found this plus twenty more cowering in a corner. Couple of them got cut up by barbed wire. The shooter got them all in the head. Had to be a good shot."

He walked through the gate and to each dead animal, kicked the ground. Cursed and nearly jumped out of his skin when his phone rang. He jerked it out of his pocket, relieved when Dianne's number flashed on the screen. "Dianne, where are you?"

"What's wrong? We've been at the early matinee and our phones were off."

"Someone shot up a pasture full of heifers, killed ten of them. Whoever did it was a crack shot. We're waiting on Sam out here. Go home. Lock every door. Call me when you're there and leave your phones on."

* * * *

Dianne slid down the wall of the theater lobby. Simon was behind this. He was losing control of his persona, more dangerous than ever. "That was Kip. Someone's killed ten of his heifers. He said to go home and lock up."

Jocelyn helped Dianne up and took her to the car. "Give me the keys."

Dianne handed her purse to Jocelyn. "Simon is behind this. But how? Sam's checking on it and will probably alert the local police."

"Where there's an evil will, there's a way. What did you ever see in that man?"

"That's what I've asked myself a thousand times."

* * * *

Kip couldn't stand still. He kicked rocks, hurled stones, and cursed. "Ricochet, take some pictures with your phone. I reckon Sam will want some. Me, I want to take the photos and pile them up around Simon's feet then set fire to the bastard."

When Sam pulled up, he was putting his cell phone in his pocket. "I just talked to the detectives. Simon's been at his hotel all day. What happened?"

"The guys came out to check on the heifers and found this." Kip swept his outstretched arm toward the pasture littered with carcasses. "They were shot from a distance. The shooter is good. More like a sniper. Simon may not have done the shooting, but I guarantee he had something to do with it."

Sam photographed the carnage. "Show me where you saw that flash of light."

Kip pointed to the hills in the west. "It was just the one time I saw it. I didn't hear anything."

Sam shook his head and squeezed Kip's shoulder. "I'll get someone out here to look for shell casings and anything else that might have been left behind. Don't expect to find much but can't ever tell. A trained sniper wouldn't leave anything behind. A hired thug might be a little more careless. And it doesn't take a rocket scientist to use a silencer. You can go ahead and take care of these heifers."

* * * *

When they arrived home, Jocelyn went in to take a bath.

Restless and worried, Dianne gathered a book and lap blanket then informed Jocelyn she was headed to the basement. The cool temperature and musty scent melded together to create an atmosphere of age and history that permeated every nook and cranny. The last set of stairs led to a room dominated wall-to-wall by an oak bar. She stopped for a moment to absorb the ambiance.

Several small tables and groups of chairs sat spaced out to encourage conversation when the space was used for special events. Two main rooms branched off into four smaller ones. Marble gargoyles served as sentries over each doorway. Italian tiles covered the floors. The library, with its stacks of century-old law books, leather bound novels, files, and leather sofas, made the basement another favorite area for her.

Over the years, the mansion and basement had served many purposes. A private home. Rooms for servants. An upscale restaurant. A speakeasy bar. An antique market and several business offices.

She flipped on a light and gasped. The book and blanket she carried tumbled to the floor. A black sable coat she had left at Simon's when they divorced lay across the sofa.

A chill raced through her, stopping her heart. She screamed when a man appeared in the doorway. He had a scruffy beard and wore overalls with a plaid shirt. An unlit cigar hung from the corner of his mouth.

"Who are you?" The words came out in a choked whisper.

"Name's Larry. And, I have a little surprise for you."

Before she could react, he'd crossed the room, grabbed her, and clamped a hand over her mouth.

"You and me gonna take a little ride. I know someone anxious to see you."

Oh, God. Would Jocelyn come down to look for her? How long would she have to be gone before her friend became concerned?

The man pulled her toward the door. She struggled and tried to bite his hand, but her little moves were of no use compared to his larger, stronger frame. Her only hope was that someone would find her…before it was too late.

* * * *

Kip's phone rang. Jocelyn's name flashed on the screen. Fear and dread skittered up his back. "Hey. Is something wrong?"

"I think so. I don't know. Something is going on. Dianne went down to the basement to relax not long after she last talked to you. She was down there longer than I thought she would be, so I went to check on her. She's not there." Jocelyn voice cracked.

"Calm down. What makes you think she's gone? Maybe she's walking in the yard."

"A fur coat that Simon gave her years ago was tossed across the sofa. She'd left it with him when she filed for divorce. And her book and blanket were on the floor. The back door to the maintenance room is open. Sometimes the gardener leaves it that way, but I really believe Simon is here or its someone working for him." Jocelyn's voice shook with panic.

Kip swallowed the bile rising in his throat. He clutched his chest. His heart sped up to lightning speed then lurched to a stop before beating once again. Fear left him sweating and shaking. He inhaled sharply and moved the phone between his jaw and shoulder.

"He's hired someone. She's gone." Jocelyn's calm dissolved into shuddering sobs.

"Stay put. I'm coming. I'll bring Sam with me. In the meantime, call the Wichita Falls Police Department. Don't touch anything. We'll get her back." Kip dropped the phone in his shirt pocket. He would kill Simon Jacobson.

Chapter 19

A nondescript black rental car waited outside a gate shrouded by magnolia trees showing off creamy blossoms and heavy, deep green leaves. Dianne caught the sweet fragrance as Larry shoved her into the car. At first, she was too angry to be frightened. Determined not to cry, she gritted her teeth, swallowed hard, and focused on where the car was headed.

Fifteen minutes later, they pulled into a small air strip. Dianne recognized Simon's private jet waiting on the tarmac. A surge of fear replaced the fiery anger that had simmered in her thoughts. Fear and uncertainty burned the back of her throat. She coughed. "What's going on? Is Simon in that plane?"

"Taking a little trip to New York City. And no, Simon isn't on the plane.

"But Simon's here."

"Not anymore. He gave those yokels the slip. He's waiting for his lovely bride—that would be you—in New York City." Larry started laughing at the situation. He doubled over, gripped his sides, and stomped his feet.

Despair clutched her stomach. Would Kip come all the way to New York to find her? Would he figure out she had been kidnapped or would he believe she betrayed him again? In that moment she knew as sure as summer rain, she would never willingly return to her former life. Her home was here . . . her heart was here. Too late for her and Kip or not, she would return home when this was all over.

If I live through it.

* * * *

Dianne looked out the window as the plane began its descent at a private airport. Panic stirred despite her best efforts. She rubbed her chest and tried to use calming breaths.

Larry pulled a phone from his pocket. Dianne listened as he informed Simon of their arrival. *I will stay alert and aware. I'll do whatever I must do to keep Kip and my friends safe.*

The plane taxied slowly to the only open hanger. Not knowing what the next few hours held in store for her caused every part of her body to fight for centerstage attention. Simon was cruel. She had to stay on guard and be as calm as possible.

The attendant on the tarmac lowered the steps. Larry led the way. Dianne followed. She sensed Simon's presence and saw him waiting beneath an awning. He smiled and waved as if she were returning home from a business trip. She refused to acknowledge him until she could look him in the eye.

"Welcome home, sweetheart. How was your trip? I trust the flight went well." Simon chuckled.

Dianne pulled her shoulders back, held her chin up, and crossed her arms across her chest. She narrowed her eyes in a defiant stare. "I'm not your sweetheart. Why am I here?"

"I decided not to deal with those hicks in Oklahoma and Texas anymore. You are supposed to be here with me. Divorce was never my option. We will marry again in two days. It's been arranged." Simon reached for her elbow and led her through the small airport.

Dianne jerked her arm away and stepped to the side. Even a few inches distance from him felt safer. She tried to edge farther away, but Larry closed up the space. *Trapped!*

Not for long.

A luxurious town car with a tuxedoed valet waited at the door. She stopped and whirled around to face Simon. "Why did you have Kip's heifers shot?"

"Why not? I had to get your attention somehow. Besides, a few cows aren't significant."

"Really? Think again. Cattle are important to ranchers. Those heifers you had shot were worth about ten thousand dollars without figuring in their added worth when they became old enough to breed and have calves."

"Well, then, I guess it was a good choice. Your cowboy might think twice before causing trouble for me. I was here. Just ask Larry. Nobody saw him, so how can anyone prove I had anything to do with it? Now, let's get you home and into some decent clothes. You won't ever wear jeans and western shirts again. Or those cowboy boots. Nor will you ever ride a horse." Simon ran his hand up and down Dianne's arm.

She jerked away, stopped midstride, and turned her back on him, knowing Simon always hated it when she didn't look him in the eye. "Oh, someone will figure this out. You will be sorry. As far as my clothes are concerned, you have no say."

"But I do. You got here without the benefit of being able to get any of your own things including your license, passport, and credit cards. Leaves you rather helpless and dependent on me, doesn't it?"

Helpless, yes—for now—but not yet hopeless. Dianne scooted as far from Simon as possible until the seat belt tightened, and she couldn't move away. "I have a passport and identification. Did you believe I would be so stupid as to not have those things available?"

The drive through New York City traffic shattered her nerves. Defeat overwhelmed her, yet she maintained a perfect posture of society with her shoulders stiff and her back straight. For her it demonstrated courage. When they arrived at Simon's apartment building, she exited the car with poise and grace. She smiled and spoke to the familiar doorman. The private elevator sped to the penthouse, leaving her gut at the bottom.

"For now, my dear, I have arranged for you to sleep in the spare bedroom. You'll find clothes in the closet and luxury toiletries in the bath. There is no phone in that room. The doorman knows not to allow anyone up at all. Now, go bathe and dress for dinner. We're going out."

His phone rang. He rolled his eyes with a long-suffering sigh. "Simon Jacobson."

Dianne watched the expressions cross Simon's face. Smugness, anger, then amusement. He ended the call with a sadistic chuckle.

"The smalltown sheriff said he's having officers check your apartment for evidence of wrongdoing. They haven't found anything, so he said. Truth is, they won't find anything. I imagine he's trying to scare me a bit. He doesn't know that I don't get scared. By the way, your friends Kip and Jocelyn are flying out here. That bunch of country idiots don't know who they're messing with. I think I'm going to enjoy watching this whole thing fall apart on them." Simon laughed and clapped his hands.

"Don't hurt them. I'll do whatever you wish. I'll tell them to go back home, that I want to be with you." Dianne's voice shook. Her hands shook. Fear rampaged through her body, leaving her cold and faint. Her courage failed her. She collapsed to the floor.

Simon gave Dianne his phone. "Talk to him."

Her mind went blank. She couldn't recall the number. Her fingers shook so hard it took three tries for her to finally remember to just hit 'redial.'

"Hello. Sheriff Sam Walker speaking."

"Sam, please stay there. Don't come. Don't let Kip or Jocelyn come. I'll be all right. Simon admitted to having a man named Larry kill the heifers and kidnap me." She ended the call before Sam could respond.

Simon slapped her across the face so hard her neck whip-lashed, and the phone flew across the room. Tears sprang to her eyes, her skin stung, and she rubbed her burning cheeks. The satisfaction that she had given Sam some information offered a small sense of victory.

Simon jerked her up by the arm. Hard. Dianne grabbed her shoulder, wondering if he'd dislocated it. He pushed her toward the bedroom door. "No more calls. Get in there and get dressed. Now!"

Dianne stood in the middle of the room, unable to move. She wiped her eyes with the back of her hand and opened the closet. An entire wardrobe of designer dresses, suits, coats, shoes, and bags were arranged by color. She slid some garments along the rod, clutched as many as possible, and tossed them to the floor. She chose a green cashmere sweater and black slacks from the floor, ran a brush through her hair, and left the room.

"That's much better but you must change to an evening gown for dinner and the theater. Wear the blue." Simon ordered.

Dianne held her shoulders back, jutted her chin out, and glared at him, hoping the fear building in her gut wasn't evident. "You are in no position to order me to do anything. I will do nothing more and nothing less than it takes to get away from you. Legally, you have no right to me. What you are doing is committing a blatant kidnapping along with a multitude of other broken laws."

* * * *

The plane carrying Kip, Ricochet, Sam, Jocelyn, and a Wichita Falls detective touched down. Two officers of the New York City police department met them on the tarmac.

Kip stepped aside as the law enforcement officials made introductions then moved to greet them. "It's nice to meet you. Thank you for helping. I'm Kip Mahan, Dianne's . . . friend. Do you know where she is?"

"Well, sir, we know where Mr. Jacobson's penthouse is and assume she's there. We have to go to the precinct to acquire warrants. It would be best if you and your friends stayed at a hotel. The sheriff and detective can ride along."

"Damn, I need to see her. Make sure she isn't hurt." Kip paced.

Sam put his hand on Kip's shoulder. "I know. Let us handle it. We have evidence that links Simon to several crimes. His friend, Larry, is in the system on several charges and he left fingerprints at the crime scene. Just wait. Keep your phone near and we'll get things done."

Kip nodded and tried to swallow the obstruction in his throat that prevented any cleansing breath. He tilted his head back, searching for the sun and sky, both hidden by the too-tall concrete skyline. "I can't stand this. That SOB will pay for this. If he hurts her, I'll kill him."

Sam led Kip away. "Come on, Buddy. Don't say anything you might regret. Let the law handle it. Go find something to eat and wait at the hotel."

* * * *

Dianne woke up and looked around the room. She lay still beneath a goose-down comforter, trying to remember where she was. The morning sun streamed through the eastern window and the sounds of heavy traffic, impatient drivers, and frustrated pedestrians slammed into her consciousness.

Simon is in the other room.

The memory, along with the reality that Kip and Sam were in danger, spurred her into action. She rolled over and got up. Jerking on a white silk bathrobe lying at the foot of the bed, she opened the door and marched down to the kitchen.

"Good morning, Darling." Simon smiled at her before handing her a cup of coffee.

She took the fragile Old Country Roses china cup and saucer in shaking hands. Coffee splashed over the edge of the cup, missed the saucer, and spilled on the white carpet.

Simon dropped a cloth napkin over the spill. "I thought I would go into the office for a couple of hours, then pick you up and spend the afternoon in Central Park. Since you seem to care so much about horses, we can take a carriage ride. Doesn't that sound lovely?" Simon sipped his coffee.

"Whatever you say. You should know that those carriage horses aren't properly cared for, many of them end being sold to kill pens." Dianne refused to smile at him. She gripped the cup. Anger built in her chest so full and fast she wanted to throw the hot brew in his face.

"Why would I give a damn about some old nags?" The buzzer from the front lobby rang. Simon answered it. "What?"

"Sir, the New York City police are on their way up to your apartment. I couldn't stop them."

Simon grasped Dianne with both hands and squeezed her shoulders so hard she felt the sting and stain of bruising begin. "Go to your room. Take your coffee and be quiet."

Dianne grinned. "Looks like you're in trouble."

Simon slapped her hard across the face. Hot coffee spilled and scalded her hand. Spots clouded her vision and a thousand fire ants burrowed in her cheek.

She lifted her head and stared at him. "I will not leave. What are you going to do with cops right outside your door?"

Simon jerked her so close she could smell the coffee on his breath. "Do what I say. Now! Unless you want more of your lover's animals dead. You think Larry is the only person I pay to do my bidding?"

She clenched her teeth and whirled, stalked to the room, and slammed the door just as the doorbell rang. She opened the door a crack and peered into the living room. Simon's actions and lack of clear thinking led her to believe he was more unstable than she ever imagined. She knew he was egotistical and narcissistic, but not this violent. How could she have missed it?

Simon opened the door. He stood just outside of the threshold. "Can I help you, Officer?"

"Yes, sir. We're looking for Geneva Dianne Raborn Jacobson and have reason to believe she's here."

Sam moved into Simon's line of sight when the officer spoke to him. "How'do, Simon?"

"Officer, I have no idea where Dianne is. As you know, she left here several months ago and returned to her hometown. Is she missing?"

"You know damn well she's missing, you sorry SOB." Sam bulldozed past Simon.

"Wait. You cannot enter my home."

"Sure, we can. The officer there has a warrant to search your home, office, and the home of a street thug named Larry Soileau."

Simon jerked the warrant out of the officer's hand. He examined it and moved to sit on the entryway chair.

Dianne stepped out of the bedroom fully dressed. She ran to her friend. "Sam! I knew you would come. Is Kip safe? Is Jocelyn safe?"

"Yeah. They're both safe and waiting to see you."

"How did you find me?"

"We suspected Simon. Larry got sloppy and left fingerprints in the basement and on the shell casings at the ranch. He's been picked up and already copped to being hired by Simon. He has audios of conversations and some written instructions."

Simon glared at Dianne as he was cuffed and read his Miranda Rights. "I'll be out by tonight. Don't let your guard down. I'll be back to get you."

"I didn't do this to you. I didn't humiliate you. You did that to yourself."

The officer jerked Simon's hands behind his back and tightened the cuffs. "I wouldn't talk much if I were you. Crossing state lines. Kidnapping. Destruction of property. Anything else?"

Simon roared and jerked away from the policeman. "I want your full name and badge number. I will have you fired."

"Not likely, sir."

* * * *

Kip tried to relax with Jocelyn and Ricochet in the hotel restaurant. He checked his watch repeatedly. *My God, what is making time drag on?* His ability to concentrate had fled. He rubbed his hands on the front of his jeans.

"Well, I'll be damned. Will you look at that?" Ricochet socked Kip in the arm, smiled, and stood.

Kip and Jocelyn turned to see Dianne walk through the door. Tears flowed unchecked down her face.

Kip jumped to his feet, knocking the chair to the floor, and broke into a run. Scooping Dianne up in his arms, he kissed her. Her soft lips against his was the most amazing feeling in the world. What would he have done if he'd lost her?

When they broke the kiss, Dianne looked past him to Jocelyn who sobbed into a shredded tissue.

Dianne moved to her friend and put her arms around her. "Hey. It's okay. I'm going to be just fine."

"I'm sorry. I should never have let you go down to the basement. He hit you, didn't he?" Jocelyn touched Dianne's bruised cheek.

Anger flashed in Kip's eyes when he saw the bruise. He reached over and touched it. "He'll never come near you again."

"It doesn't matter. I'm safe now. How could you have known what was going to happen? I'm thankful that I was only here for two days before y'all found me. Fast work for all of you. I'll be forever grateful."

Kip slipped an arm around her waist. He didn't want to stop touching her, reassuring himself she was here . . . she was real. "We need to wait on the detectives, and Sam, of course, before heading home. But it shouldn't take long. Who knows about this kind of thing? I think Sam is going to have Simon extradited to Waurika for the cattle. The Wichita Falls department has an arrest warrant for the kidnapping. Simon's going to fight it, I reckon. His status won't matter much where we're from."

Jocelyn turned to Ricochet. "Hey, how about we take a walk to take in some sights? Leave these two alone for a while and let them talk."

Ricochet frowned. "What's there to see here but tall buildings, traffic, and people?"

Jocelyn laughed. She looped her arm through his and led him to the door. "Oh, you might be surprised."

* * * *

Kip turned to Dianne. "Maybe we should go somewhere more private. I've got a room upstairs."

Dianne nodded. "Sounds perfect."

The elevator cables creaked, mimicking her beating heart. She felt relief and elation riding up, but a sense of dread overshadowed it. Kip seemed happy to see her. She hoped he still wanted her in his life. *I want to have my say before he has a chance to set me loose. Maybe I'm wrong. It's just nerves.*

He stopped in front of room four-thirteen, opened the door, and motioned her inside.

She turned as he shut the door behind them. He started to speak, but she put a finger over his lips. "Before you say a word, I have some things I have to say to you. I have missed you terribly. All these years, I never stopped loving you. I regretted my choice many times, but sometimes I felt accomplished and that took the sting away."

"I miss—"

"I need to finish. I know I don't deserve your trust or your forgiveness, but I promise I will do everything I can to earn it. I love you." She drew in a deep breath.

Kip crossed his arms over his chest and watched her with narrowed eyes. Waiting. What was he thinking? His expression didn't reveal even a hint of emotion. Dianne touched his cheek.

"Anyway, being back in New York, even under these circumstances, made me realize this is not, nor has it ever been, the place for me. I was never truly happy here. All I want is to be back in Waurika and Wichita Falls—with or without you—but I would be happier with you." Silence stretched between them. "Well, aren't you going to say something?"

He grinned. "So, now I have permission to talk?"

She nodded.

Kip stepped closer and took her upper arms in his hands. He pulled her to him and pressed his lips against her hair. "I missed you too. I love you too, and I can never be truly happy without you. I held onto the mistrust, bitterness, and other pain because I was afraid of being hurt again. But I didn't know what fear was until I thought you wouldn't be able to come back to me. I never want to lose you again."

Tears of pure joy rose in her throat. She tilted back to look directly into his eyes. "Do you have any idea how happy you've just made me?"

"Hopefully, as happy as you make me." He bent his head and claimed her lips with his.

Her anxiety fled like geese flying south for the winter.

* * * *

Simon sat alone, dumbfounded to be in a jail cell. A man of his stature! Fear tightened his gut in rolling spasms. The rough fabric of the jumpsuit made him itch. He considered firing his team of attorneys. *Inept bastards.* He stood and grasped the cold, steel bars. "Guards! Guards! I demand to speak to someone in charge."

A burly guard sauntered to the cell and hit Simon's knuckles with a wooden baton. "You don't get to speak to anyone. You're in here until you make bail. I imagine you'll do that, but it won't take long before you'll be making your new home in the big boy prison. I figured a big-ass lawyer like you would know that kidnapping across state lines was really bad."

Simon growled. "I insist on speaking to someone who knows what the hell is going on. I've had threats made against my life. I'll own you when I get out of here."

"Everybody's had threats in this joint. Sit down, shut up, and bide your time. You're in solitary. No one will get at you. Not saying they won't try. Hell, some guard might try to get to you because you're so damned arrogant." The guard laughed and walked away.

Simon listened to the jeers of the inmates near his cell who'd heard the exchange. He paced back and forth. For the first time he knew what animals in the zoo felt like. Caged. Helpless. On display. He didn't like it at all. His mind worked in circles, but nothing made sense. Someday he would make everyone pay for this humiliation. His heart raced so fast he couldn't draw a breath into his tight chest. A heart attack might be a blessing, he thought, even as the world went black.

Chapter 20

Three weeks later Dianne walked with Kip to the barn, the shock of Simon's death diminished by the white twinkling lights illuminating the walkway between rows of stalls. Several horses slept in the corners, groomed and well-fed. The lights shimmered off the horses' coats. Emperor stretched his neck over the gate, his ears pointed toward her, and nickered.

"There's my boy. I have treats for you." Dianne rubbed his face and scratched his ears. She put her forehead to his forelock. Loving this horse was easy. He calmed her with his big, gentle presence.

"Dianne?" Kip put his arm around her waist.

"Hmm?"

"Do you remember the foal Honeybee had just before you left?"

Dianne wondered where this conversation was headed. She frowned and wrinkled her forehead. "Sure, I do. He was a feisty little thing."

Kip pushed straw to the side with his boot. "I've been waiting fifteen years to give you your graduation gift. You're giving him sugar right now. Emperor is that colt. He's all yours. I know you've said a few times you wished he was yours."

She didn't know what to think or say. "Really?"

"Yeah, really." Kip grinned and rocked back on his boot heels.

Dianne squealed, causing Emperor to toss his head back with a whinny. She flung herself into Kip's arms. "Thank you. How could I ever thank you enough? I don't deserve a gift this grand. It's the best thing I've ever received. Are you sure?"

Kip caught her by the waist, lifted her, and spun her around. "Check out his halter."

Dianne opened the stall gate and walked under Emperor's neck. "Let's see, he has a new halter. It's purple. Still my favorite color. Wait, there's a purple ribbon tied to it. I don't understand." She stepped back, puzzled.

"It's the rest of your graduation gift." Kip waited.

She reached to untie the ribbon. An emerald ring, her birthstone, was tied to it. She cried. "Oh, my God. I can't accept this. It's too much."

Kip settled his hands on Dianne's shoulders. "I bought this ring fifteen years ago. Saved two years for it. Will you finally marry me?"

"Yes. Yes, but only if you forgive me and trust me."

"I forgave you the first time I saw you at the center. I never stopped loving you. How about a midnight ride?"

Dianne pressed her lips to his ear. "I've got a better idea. Let's head to the house and go upstairs."

THE END

About the Author

Winona Bennett Cross lives in Durant, Oklahoma with her husband and is a member of the Central Region Oklahoma Writers, the Oklahoma Romance Writer's Guild, the Oklahoma Writer's Federation Inc., and the Romance Writers of America.

She has two sons and two extraordinary granddaughters plus a finicky and fussy gray tabby cat named Angus.

Nona's heart lies in the desert and oil fields of west Texas and southeast New Mexico where she was raised. In 1969 she graduated from high school in Lovington, New Mexico.

Nursing was the dream Nona achieved until a fall in the hospital abruptly ended her career. The pain of the loss remains embedded in her soul. She began experimenting with writing in 2002. Finally, in 2014 she realized she could write and tell a story and began writing in earnest.

Winona enjoys hearing from others, she can be reached at:
Nona143writer@yahoo.com

Visit Nona's Website and blog at:
https://winonabennettcross.com

Sign up to receive her newsletter to receive updates on future books!

Other Books by Winona Bennett Cross

Rebecca's Journey

Determined to keep a vow made to her dying father, independent eighteen-year-old Rebecca Pierce sets out on a wagon train on the Oregon Trail in 1845 with her mother. Rebecca is strong and takes on a leadership role.

Zachary Miller is traveling alone with nothing more than what he can carry and his horse. He is assigned to help Rebecca and her mother from the first day on the trail. Zachary falls fast for Rebecca, but she is conflicted about her growing feelings.

When Rebecca is kidnapped by an obsessive man, she is left injured, in pain, depressed, and losing the belief she had in herself.

Zachary is angry and wants revenge. He feels like there is nothing he can do to help Rebecca although he tries to do all he can.

Will their newly developed relationship recover and allow them to regain their growing love?

Rebecca's Journey is available in eBook and Print @ Amazon and other online retailers.